a novel

The Cottage

By Sara Moffitt

Order this book online at www.trafford.com
or email orders@trafford.com

Most Trafford titles are also available at major online book retailers.

Note for Librarians: A cataloguing record for this book is available from Library
and Archives Canada at www.collectionscanada.ca/amicus/index-e.html

Printed in Victoria, BC, Canada.

ISBN: 978-1-4269-2549-8

*Our mission is to efficiently provide the world's finest, most comprehensive book publishing
service, enabling every author to experience success. To find out how to publish your book, your
way, and have it available worldwide, visit us online at www.trafford.com*

Trafford rev. 03/8/10

www.trafford.com

North America & international
toll-free: 1 888 232 4444 (USA & Canada)
phone: 250 383 6864 ♦ fax: 812 355 4082

NEW BEGINNINGS

IT ALL BEGAN ONE day while I was driving my little truck on vacation. I was looking around for a small town where I could settle down, mainly because I just wanted to get away from big city life. There was just no peace and quiet or love in the city where I lived. Crime was bad, and no one seemed to care about anyone else, like it should be.

No, I was not running away from life, I was looking for a *better* life, where I could work on my talents without being disturbed. If any of you are like I am, once you start concentrating on something, you don't want to be interrupted. It's hard to get back to it with your full attention.

For a long time I wanted so badly to raise chickens and other animals, without the city saying it's against the law. I owned a golf cart and liked to drive it around town. It's better because it does not pollute the air. But they don't allow this, and you can't drive it in the streets without a driver's license. It's rules like these that take your freedom away from you in a big city.

Well, that's why I thought it would be a good idea to find a small rural town as I was driving along, enjoying the beauty of the countryside. I had just started my trip the day before, and was deeply in thought about the search.

Suddenly, I saw a billboard in a field on the right side of the highway. I pulled over to read the sign

COME VISIT OUR TOWN IN WELCOME HOME
Population 700 on property of over 11,700 acres of land
Just follow the arrow and you are there

"Wow. This is worth a side trip to check it out," I told myself. I decided to follow the arrow pointing towards town. I did not want to miss the quaint little town, so I drove slowly down so as not to miss it.

When I drove through this town, I could see that it had exactly what I was looking for. They had one of everything that I needed. They had a family food store, a yardage store, a hardware store, a beauty shop, and so forth. Up ahead was a bed-and-breakfast, an older house with a wonderful, old-fashioned wrap-around porch and rocking chairs.

I said, "This is for me." I stopped my truck at the curb, turned off the engine and set the hand brake. I climbed out and walked up the steps to the front door. The door had an upper and a lower opening to it, and was painted bright red. The name of this bed-and-breakfast was *Pleasant Dreams*. I discovered later that they had two inns in town. The other was named *Shady Acres*, at the other end of town.

I said to myself, "How clever." I knocked on the door and a sweet elderly lady answered. She had a sparkle in her eyes that drew you in and made you feel welcome and loved. She said, "Welcome to *Pleasant Dreams*. Yes, we do have a room available. Come on in."

I walked in as the lady held the door open for me. I signed the register and paid for two days. Here I was at last, in this delightful place, and it felt good. The lady said her name was Margie. I shook her hand and gave her my name as well.

"I'm Mary, and I am so glad to meet you." To my joy, this was the place I had dreamed about and had hoped to stay at for a long time during my travels. This bed-and-breakfast had seven guest rooms, all on one level, with a large entry hall. To the right was the dining room, and a kitchen lay beyond that. To the left was a living room with a piano. The other side of the living room was a library that you could go into and read if you wished.

Margie showed me around to the guest rooms and the names above each of the doors were very clever. They all had the names of flowers. There was a room called Honeysuckle. This room was painted a soft yellow, and it had a floral wallpaper border with the honeysuckle design. In the room were a white, full-sized, four-poster bed and a small desk in the corner for writing letters. There was a dressing table and a comfortable chair to sit in, where you could either read a book or look out the window at the view of her garden. None of the rooms had any television, the reason being, you could relax better without hearing about the mundane problems all over the world.

The names of the other guest room were: Sunflower, Magnolia, Geranium, Pansy, Sweet-Pea, and Lilac. Margie mentioned that breakfast was served at 8:30 AM, and on Sunday, they had a late afternoon supper for the guests.

The thing that I liked best about the inn was that it was a close walk into town. I then brought my luggage to my room, and took a shower in one of the two bathrooms shared by everyone. Then I went to my room and took a nap because I had been driving a long time and was tired.

When I woke up, it was late afternoon, so I got up, got dressed, and put on my walking shoes, then grabbed my sweater and my purse and was off to explore the town of Welcome Home.

It was a beautiful afternoon, and the air felt refreshing. As I walked, I came to a diner called Nature's Bounty. I was hungry, not having eaten since breakfast. It was now nearly evening and time for supper. As I opened the door and walked inside, I looked around for a nice place to sit.

A waitress came up to me and said, "Welcome to Nature's Bounty. My name is Cindy." She seated me at a table with a view of the town square, and then gave me a menu to ponder while she went to bring me a glass of water. I looked at all of the wonderful selections and found it hard to decide what I wanted. I settled on meatloaf, and with it came a choice of salad or soup and a small dessert and beverage.

While waiting for my meal, I noticed the diner was very busy. It was a Friday night. Some people got up to for their meal and then came over to me and introduced themselves. After they left, I felt truly welcome. The waitress brought me my meal and I enjoyed it very much. The meat loaf came with mashed potatoes, brown gravy and peas on the side, plus a dinner roll and iced tea. My salad was mixed greens, and for dessert I had raspberry sherbet.

After I was finished eating, I got up and left a nice tip, and then paid for my meal. It was 5:30 PM. I had passed an hour at the diner. The sky was now starting to show the colors of evening just before it gets dark. I knew I could only visit a couple more places before I called it a day.

As I was walking on the wooden sidewalk, I noticed a cute bookstore named *Your Mind's an Adventure*. To me, that really fit into what reading is all about. I opened the door and a tiny bell announced my entry. The store had a wonderful collection on many topics. As I was browsing through the stacks, all of a sudden a book fell off the shelf into my hands. The book was called *Sweet Mysteries of Life*. I took my book to the cashier and paid the lady for the book.

She said, "Well, hello. Are you new in town?"

I said, "Yes. I was on vacation, and turned off of the highway because of the name on a billboard, and the name kind of called out to me."

She said, "Yes, a lot of visitors have said the same thing. I am so sorry. Let me introduce myself. My name is Jill."

Then I told her my name was Mary. As we talked I told her I was looking for a place to stay, and told her what I had in mind.

Her eyes lit up with delight. She said, "Wow. This may sound strange, but I have been expecting you. You truly have come to the right place, for our town just so happens to have an empty cottage not far from here. It has been waiting for a long time for the right owner." She explained further. "The owner of the hardware store a couple of buildings down from my store is the owner of the cottage, if you would like to talk to him."

I said thank you to Jill and went on my way. When I got to the hardware store, which had the name *Handy Tools*, they were just getting ready to close. The manager's name was Hank. Hank said he was about to close and wanted to know how he could help me.

I gave him my name, then said "Jill at the book store mentioned you have a cottage for sale."

He said, "Yes, this cottage really needs a loving person to take care of her, if you are interested. Come back tomorrow morning at 10:00 AM and we will talk, and I will take you over to the cottage, so you can look and see what you think."

It was growing dark as I said goodbye and walked back to the inn. I went to my room and got ready for bed. I needed a good night's sleep after all the driving. I had a big day tomorrow, and also many things to learn about this new town.

I awoke to birds singing their greetings for a brand new day. I got up and occupied the bathroom before the other guests were up, then went back to my room and got dressed before going to breakfast. I sat down and said my prayers, and by then it was time for breakfast.

The aroma was so inviting as I entered the dining room. The side board had blueberry muffins, eggs, bacon and sausage to choose from, and freshly squeezed orange juice, coffee and tea. When I was done eating, I thanked Margie for the wonderful breakfast and took my new book with me to the front porch and read for a while. It was still early, and my appointment wasn't until 10:00 AM. I was so excited about being shown the cottage that it was hard for me to concentrate on the book, so I just sat and rocked in the chair for a while, and enjoyed the morning.

I was in my reverie and it felt good. I looked at my watch and saw it was almost time to leave, so I took my book back to my room, then walked to town. I was a few minutes early, but that was okay, for I would rather be early than late. In this town, the sidewalks were raised with railings. There was a wooden bench outside Handy Tools, so I sat down to wait for the store's owner.

Soon Hank, the owner, drove up, and he opened the door to his store and we walked inside. He gave me a chair to sit in, and got one for himself too. He told me the story about the cottage.

"Many years ago," said Hank, "a sweet lady had this built for her, and it fit who she was to a tee. She put a lot of love into this with all of her flowers and trees, and many other things. When anyone came to visit her, you could feel pure love and belonging. But I won't say any more, for you need to see for yourself."

Hank's young helpers came in the door just then, so he told them that he would be gone for a while to show me the cottage. We then got into his small truck and were on our way. The cottage was about a mile out of town, on three acres. It took a lot of room with all that the past owner had placed on the grounds of her home.

Soon we were there, and Hank parked his truck, turned off the motor, and set the hand brake, then got out of the truck, came around to the passenger side, and opened the door for me. I climbed down and was escorted to the cottage.

When I saw it, my mouth dropped open, and tears began to fall from my eyes down my cheeks, because it was exactly what I had dreamed about so many times.

Hank looked at me and said, "Are you all right?"

I said, "Yes, I am very all right. These are tears of joy because I had a dream about this very cottage a long time ago, and it has everything I dreamed about. This is what I saw in my dream."

The cottage was Irish with a thatched roof. To get to it, there was a bridge over a small river, with an arbor leading to the front door on a curving stone walkway. The small river wound around the cottage to the back side of it, and kept going to the main river. All around this cottage were all kinds of flowers and garden benches to sit on. In the back was a lot of space to grow fruit trees. There was a place to raise chickens as well. There was also a guest house made to look like the main cottage. There was also a barn, so this was perfect for me.

Back in the front yard, I could see that the small river came from another direction, from the river above the cottage. I knew then and there that I would buy this cottage. I wanted this cottage very badly. So I set the deal and made out a check for the full amount. I had been saving for this cottage for many years. I just happened to have the full amount Hank needed for this lovely cottage.

After that, we drove back to town with hearts of joy because Hank found a buyer, and I found my dream home. When we got to the hardware store, I gave Hank a big hug, which made his face turn red. He told me that on Sundays, the stores were not open, for this was a day of rest.

I asked, "Is the town allowed golf carts to drive in town?"

He said, "Yes, and you don't have to have a license to drive your golf cart."

I then went back to the inn and told Margie what had happened, and we were both happy. I told Margie that I would be checking out today because I had to drive home and start packing my things, so I could move into the cottage as soon as possible. We said our goodbyes, and Margie fixed me a lunch to eat on my drive home.

When I finally got home after three and a half days, I went and picked up my dog and birds. I didn't need to feed them just yet, for they had already been fed. Since I had just gotten home, I relaxed and read all of my mail. When this was done, I got up and fixed supper, fed my dog named Sparkle and gave her fresh water. Then I took a shower and got ready for bed. I said my prayers, and got in bed. It was Wednesday when I arrived home. I only had four more days until I had to go back to work.

I woke up bright and early Thursday morning, and took my dog for a walk, then came home and fed the dog and my birds, and had a big breakfast of sausage and three eggs and toast and coffee. After breakfast, I called my landlord to give him a thirty-day notice. The landlord was sorry to learn I was moving, but was happy that I had found a nice place and a new life. It was the end of November, and I was leaving at the end of December, into the new year.

I got dressed and put my dog in the backyard while I went to town to look for packing boxes. I only had Friday to Sunday to start on my packing. I had to do my best and get as much done as I was able, because on Monday I would be going back to work. I collected the boxes I needed and took them home, then started to pack the things that were not used all of the time. From Friday to Sunday I was very busy packing as much as I could, to have at least part of the packing done and out of the way.

Monday morning I went in early to my job at the book store, called *Many Journeys*, because I wanted to talk to my boss Mandy. I told Mandy that I was moving in a month and was giving her two weeks' notice. She was sad that I would be leaving, and she told me

I was a loyal worker and always on time. She gave me a hug and said she would miss me, and wished me a wonderful happy new life.

The next two weeks went as usual at the book store, and finally it was the last day. My boss gave me a going-away party and a gift — one my favorite books, called *Mystical Travels*. I then hugged everyone I worked with and left with tears in my eyes. I loved working there. You see, I was sixty-seven and ready to retire. I should have done it sooner, but I just wanted to wait a little longer.

The packing got into full swing during the month of December, even with the delays of Christmas Day with my parents. They were very pleased that I had found a nice little town to live in, and that it was a safe place for me to live.

The big moving day finally arrived on January 1st. I hired a moving company to transport all of my belongings to the town of Welcome Home. I bought a trailer hitch, and I was able to haul my golf cart behind my specially built truck, which had a camper hood on the back. It had a small truck bed. I placed my dog and birds in the back. I said goodbye, and was on a three-or four day trip to my new home. My little specially made highway-legal truck was a small truck. In the back were a sleeping bag and a camp stove and ice chest, plus food and water for the trip. The small truck was emerald green in color.

I stopped for the night at a camping ground. I took Sparkle, my golden retriever, for a walk, for she had been riding in my truck a long time. I had to drive such a long distance and knew it was hard on her. Then I fixed supper and fed my pets.

The next morning I continued driving and did the same each night and just had one more night before I arrived at my new home.

To my joy, the moving truck was at the cottage, and thanks to Hank, the movers were already unloading my things into my little cottage.

I parked my car and got the leash and put it on Sparkle, and took her around to the back, to a special fenced-in yard, and released her. Then I went back in front and got my birds out and took each cage to the sunroom inside. Then I went back to my truck and took the rest of my things out and brought them into my cottage. I placed my plants in the sunroom. As I looked out the window I saw my dog having a great time in the yard, and that made me smile.

The moving people finally finished moving all my belongings into the cottage, and we said goodbye. I thanked them for all their hard work. Then they were on their way back to the company they worked for. I also thanked Hank for guiding the moving truck.

In the next few hours I was busy getting things ready for my bed and my kitchen things put away. After that, I went into my new bedroom and took a much needed nap. When I woke up, it was dark. I let Sparkle in, fed her, and made a small supper for myself.

After eating, I cleaned up the kitchen, sat down, and just enjoyed my new home for the rest of the evening. Then I went to bed because I had a lot to do in the morning. I wanted to get as much done as I could. This way I could explore the little town on the weekend.

On Friday morning I got up early, got dressed right away, and took Sparkle for her first walk in our new home. It was wonderful to walk in the country, but the weather was cold, seeing that this was winter. It did not snow very often in this mild climate, but for some reason it just felt extra cold that morning.

We were able to walk two miles and back. As we walked, I could see the upper river that flowed to my narrow river that wound around my cottage. The trees were bare, and so I felt we just might have snow. I could see some rocky areas where there was a mountain in the distance. This would bring a great possibility for spring and summer hiking. In the distance I could make out a glittering of either a lake or maybe a waterfall, but that would have to wait.

Suddenly, the wind picked up. Sparkle and I then walked briskly back to the cottage. I was shivering as I came in the door, because I didn't have a heavy jacket on. I decided to make a fire in the fireplace. There were some small logs on a stand close by. After I got it started, I felt warmer, so I went to the kitchen and fed Sparkle and gave her water, and fixed myself a cup of hot coffee. Then I put on a sweater and sat, facing the fireplace, in a comfortable chair, and pulled a blanket from one of the unpacked boxes. I just sat there for a while to get warm. I was so cozy that I fell asleep.

That was strange, because that did not happen very often with me early in the morning. Suddenly, I was dreaming of what Sparkle and I saw on our walk. I could see the mountains and the lake in my dream, and it was as smooth as glass. As I was walking around this lake, I saw a jetty, and a small boat tied to the jetty. The boat was white with a blue stripe all the way around it, and it had two oars placed inside. Next, Sparkle and I got into the boat, and I rowed the boat away from the jetty. I found myself near the edge of a cave and I rowed inside, and — *wow* — *what a magnificent sight to behold!* There were stalactites and stalagmites, and a glow of some kind coming from behind them.

I was suddenly awake. I wondered if that was a premonition of future adventures. I guess I wouldn't know until I had a chance to check for myself in the spring or summer. I got up and made my breakfast, because I was warmer now. But from time to time I would add more wood to the fire.

After breakfast I tackled the boxes, and kept at it until everything was put away in the proper places, and then I fixed lunch. As I looked out the kitchen window, it was snowing and coming down hard. It was also beautiful at the same time. For some reason, I felt like I needed to write in my journal, and I did, because of all of the wonderful things that were going on in my life the past couple of weeks.

It was too cold to use my golf cart, so I drove my truck to town to pick up some supplies from the general store named *Larry's Market and Department store.* When I walked in, it was like a page from the past, because it had everything you needed in one store, and a round old-fashioned potbelly stove sat in the middle of the store, where the old-timers could sit and talk and just enjoy their friendship.

The owner was filling the shelves with some supplies, and turned around and asked how he could help me. This man had pure white hair and was about five feet, seven inches tall, and a little chunky from age with a jolly smile. There was a warm feeling about him.

I said "Yes, since this is my first two days living at the cottage, I felt I needed to stock up on things that I was out of, and also buy a warm jacket."

He said, "You're the new owner of the cottage that has stood empty all of these years. We are so pleased to have you in our town." Then he helped me find what I needed, since I was new to the store, and I found a nice warm jacket for myself as well. This store had things from food to dry goods for long winter days, and also old-fashioned items for anyone who canned. It also had feed for horses and cows and chickens as well.

I paid for everything I'd bought, and he had his son carry everything out to my truck for me, where he put everything in the back. As I was driving I thought I had better stop at the small post office and get some stamps and change-of-address cards, then go to the local bank, which was called *Bank One*. This was the only bank in town, by the way.

When I was there, I filled out some papers to get my funds transferred from my bank in the city where my checking and savings accounts were, so now that was done. I made a mental note in my head to go to the Motor Vehicle office on Monday, as well as the Social Security office, and file for my Social Security, since I was eligible to receive this and Medicare, although I was older than what the age limit was. Also on Monday I wanted to find a local doctor. So Monday was going to be a very busy day for me.

It was noon now, and I was hungry, so I stopped in at the diner to have some lunch. Cindy said hello, and said she was so happy to see me. She led me to a nice place to sit and gave me a menu and I told her I wanted some hot tea while I was waiting and looking to see what I wanted to eat. Cindy brought my tea, which was herbal tea, with some honey to sweeten it. On the menu I saw veggie burgers and fruit with fries on the side, so that's what I ordered.

After I ate, I paid for my lunch and left a tip, and went to one more store. The bakery was only a few steps from the diner. It had a heavy aroma of baked goods. There was so much to choose from. I chose some freshly baked bread and some bear claws for my Saturday breakfast. I got a coconut cream pie for Sunday, because I still was not in the mood to bake — not just yet. The name of the bakery was *Sweet Delights*, and the owner was a nice lady with red hair and blue eyes. Her name was Rebecca. She told me, "Welcome to our town. I'm glad to have new customer."

I thanked her and said I would be back another day, and went home. When I arrived, I unloaded my car and then put it in the garage that was built to resemble the cottage. I put everything I had bought inside and put away, then sat beside the fire, after I put more wood on it. Once I was cozy and warm again, I curled up and read my new book. This book was so interesting to read, I could not put it down —it was so exciting.

Then I looked at the clock, and it was time to fix supper. I got up, and Sparkle wanted out. I let her out to romp around for a while. Then I got real busy with cooking. What I fixed was pork chops and pan-fried potatoes, and then I made applesauce. I let Sparkle back in the house and fed her, then sat down and ate my supper. Afterwards, I did the dishes and cleaned the kitchen for the night, then took care of getting ready for bed by taking a nice bubble bath that felt so good. I dried off and put on my night clothes, then turned off the light and went to bed. I slept like a baby.

When I got up on Saturday morning, I let Sparkle out, and while she was out I cleaned out the fireplace and put the ashes in a bucket to save for the garden, then made a new fire in the fireplace. I let Sparkle back in and fed her. I made a fresh pot of coffee and just had one bear claw from the bakery with butter on it. It was satisfying to start a brand new day.

Then it occurred to me that the stores would be closed on Sunday, so I had better get some more food items. I dressed in warm clothes and put on my new jacket, hat and gloves, got my purse, put a leash on Sparkle, and then opened the garage and put her in the back of the truck. After I backed out, I got out again and closed the garage door, and then drove to town. As I was driving to town, many thoughts went through my mind, mainly because everything was happening so fast. When I approached town, I realized how much of an impact this was going to have on my new life. They didn't have parallel parking, and that was better. I left Sparkle in the truck, then went into the store and got enough things to cover my needs for a few days.

Milk and things like that get used up faster. The store's owner was very helpful and had his son carry the goods to my truck. I introduced Sparkle to Steve, and he gave her a pat on the back. She barked in greeting. I thanked Steve, then went on my way.

My next stop was the hardware store because I needed to ask some questions about where to find a builder for a chicken coop. I parked my truck and this time I put a leash on Sparkle and we both went inside. Sparkle was so glad to go with me in the store that it looked like she had a smile on her face. When I opened the door, Hank was there to greet us. He came and kneeled down to give Sparkle a pat on her head. Then he said, "She is really a sweet-natured dog. You are lucky to have her."

I said, "Yes I am. She watches over me and keeps me company."

Hank said, "What can I do for you today?"

I said, "In the spring I would like to have a chicken coop built and wanted to know if you know anyone who could build one. I want it to be big enough to house enough hens so that I have eggs enough to use to bake and for breakfast. I know that first I will need either young chicks or maybe even older ones. I am new at this. Someone has to guide me on what to do for starters."

Hank said, "Yes, I do know someone who could do this for you. He also knows a lot about chickens. Here is his address. He is outside of town, about a mile or two from here. His name is George and he has a farm."

I said, "Thank you so much, Hank. This is wonderful. I am really getting a good start on my life in this town." I said goodbye, then took care of a couple other errands.

The next stop was the beauty shop. I needed to make an appointment for Tuesday, to have my hair done. This beauty shop was called *Snip and Curl*. When I entered, the nice lady with a joyful smile said, "Hello. You are the one who bought the cottage out of town. My name is Pat."

I said, "Hello. I would like to set up an appointment for Tuesday morning at about 11:00 AM. Is there an opening?"

Pat said, "Yes, we just got one. The lady that was supposed to come had an emergency and will be out of town for a while. We also do the full works at my shop, from manicures to pedicures, if you are interested sometime. We also have seven stations here, so our ladies do not have to wait so long."

This was so nice, to have a hometown feel everywhere I went. I said to myself, "There is something very special going on in this town and hopefully I will find out the history of it sometime." I hoped there were books I could read on the town. I felt that even *this* place had a story.

I went to the library, walked in, and signed up for a library card. Then I picked out three books to read. I asked the librarian what the name of their church was.

She smiled at me and said, "Our church is more like a free worship chapel, with no one special belief, for we all have a type of universal truth that seeks the way that we are truly supposed to gather as one." Then she asked, "Would you like to come tomorrow and join us, because we would really love to have you meet us and see how we all work together."

I said, "Yes, this is truthfully what I have yearned for, in fact, for many years now. What time is your service in the morning?"

"Oh, how wonderful. The service starts at 9:00 AM. I forgot to tell you my name, didn't I? My name is Grace. What is yours?"

"My name is Mary."

Grace then said something that really surprised me. She said, "Do you know what? Our names are all very different on Earth than they are in the heavens, and our missions in life are many, for Yahweh has a special gift for us all when we go home to our true beginning."

"That is so beautiful, and, yes, I will be there on time in the morning. Thank you for helping me with these new things to think about." Before I left, I asked, "Is there a special dress code?"

Grace said, "What you wear is how you respect yourself and Yahweh."

After this enlightening morning, I left and then drove the two miles to the farm to talk to George about a chicken coop and chickens. Thank goodness he was home, and I was able to talk to him. His wife, Georgia, answered the door, and I walked into their nice farm house. I told her that Hank at the hardware store had given me the address, and I had come over after doing some errands.

She said, "We were expecting you. Hank called us and said you would be here soon." Then we all talked and George told me that in the spring he would come to my place and get to work on the chicken coop. Then we said our goodbyes.

As I was about to leave, Georgia said, "You come on over after Chapel service and have lunch with us. We would love to have you. There will be others, for this is a tradition every Sunday. It's more like pot luck."

I said, "I would love to come," and then left and drove home to my cottage.

When Sparkle and I got home, I put her outside for a while, so she could get some exercise. Then I brought all of my goods inside and put them away. I parked my truck in the garage. The fireplace had barely an ember, so I let it burn out, and turned on the heater for awhile, to warm everything up. Then I turned it off. Before I got started cooking a dish for the pot luck, I let Sparkle into the house, so she could lie down and have her rest. I checked on my birds. I had a canary and parakeets and a mynah bird. I wanted them to be warm and comfortable too.

Next, I fixed a small lunch of a bologna sandwich, tomato soup and herb tea with honey, then sat down and ate my food. Afterwards I got busy and made two Dutch apple pies and a carrot salad for the pot luck after the Chapel service.

When this was put away, I decided I really needed a nap and went to my room upstairs to lie down. This time it was like the dream from the day before was continued, because I was in the cave and saw an opening where the light was coming from. Something told me to wait before going in. "You must learn the secret of why you came here first, and when you can do this, then you will have the key to enter."

Then I woke up. This dream was really piquing my interest. There was obviously more to it than I had imagined there could be. Then a voice spoke inside my head. *"Yes, my child, what you have said is very true. You are on a quest to find out the secret of this town, and everyone in this town is a part of it. You were sent here to work with them, and you are all one. I am your guide, and we will talk again soon. But always be aware and ready, because I will need your complete attention. Much love is sent to you, my child. I am Stands with Clouds."*

Wow. This was all new to me and very exciting. I was not afraid. I honored these messages. For some reason I felt that on one of my future adventures I would check into a Native American village and find out if they could give me a DNA test, to see if I could possibly have Native American blood. But that would be for another time.

"Oh, my, it's getting time for supper. I had better get started," I said to myself. I fed Sparkle, then fixed my supper. I made salmon cakes with a white sauce, peas, and had a nice green salad and herb tea with honey. Since I was going to a pot luck tomorrow, I cut a piece of the pie I'd bought at the bakery. After I ate, I cleaned the kitchen and took a nice hot bath and washed my hair and dried it. Then I got ready for bed, climbed in and went to sleep. Sparkle came in and got comfortable on the rug beside my bed.

This night my dream was about a woman, and she was talking to me, and we were together in this beautiful place with natural crystals all around us. The crystals shone like diamonds and different gemstones. We sat together in bucket-shaped white marble chairs and she then began to talk to me.

"Dear Child, you do not remember me right now, but I am your sister from the stars. My name is Lobe and I am your other guide. You are going to the chapel in the morning, and I want you to give the following message please, because these wonderful souls need to know what is in store for them. Each will get a different message from this one, and it will be for their own growth on their path they are on now. So listen carefully and write it down for me, so you do not forget what to say.

"Beloved ones, all of you were called together in this small area of 1100 or so acres, to join together many like-minded souls as yourselves. Many more are to come who are being called at this time, many who have heard the call, one at a time. Some have varied skills, to make sure your community will stay safe from outside interference. May the joy within be humble joy and loving kindness at all times. Soon it will be revealed, the coming of a special soul to heal your mind, body and

spirit. You knew her eons ago, but you did not know her name, for she wanted to observe you first. This woman does not know it is her right now, for she has not awakened yet to her true purpose. She will know within seven years. It could be any one of you, but this you must not ask of each other. You all have so many new lessons to learn. So go with joyful hearts this special Sunday of rest. Love, Commander Lobe."

"Thank you," I said. "I will do this, and bye for now, my sister."

I woke up and fixed my breakfast, and as I looked out the kitchen window, I noticed that the sun was shining and it was a warm 65 degrees. This was very good, because I could let Sparkle stay outside while I was at the chapel and at the pot luck. I fed Sparkle, and went upstairs to get ready. This was a nice day, so I put on a pant suit that was a navy blue, with nice low-heeled navy blue shoes. The outfit had a nautical look about it. It had brass buttons on the cuffs of the jacket, and a navy blue purse.

Soon I had the ice chest filled with ice, and put the pies and large carrot salad into it. I put this in the back of my truck. I made sure Sparkle had plenty of water, then put her in the fenced-in yard. I backed out of the garage and closed the garage door, and was on my way.

The drive was so nice, going to the chapel on the top of a small hill. The drive up the winding long driveway was beautifully lined with rose bushes. When I arrived at the chapel's parking lot, there were already many cars. I parked and turned the wheels toward the curb because it was on a hill. I set the hand brake as well. As I got out and locked my truck, Grace came up to meet me and gave me a hug.

She said, "I am so happy you were able to make it today." We walked, arm in arm, to the chapel. When I finally had a look at it for the first time, my eyes nearly popped out of my head in surprise. What I saw was a glass building. There were planters throughout the inside of the chapel, with ferns growing in them and also wild orchids. Hanging not too high were brass cages of canaries singing to the organ music that was being played inside to Hawaiian music. Grace next told me that she noticed that I hadn't brought a Bible, and she was glad, because it was not needed here.

This was a very large chapel that seated many. Then it was time for the service to begin, and to my surprise, Grace was the one who gave a prayer and also a nice talk, in the form of a poem:

May the presence of Yahweh be a song in your hearts.
May he build your energy to the top of the hill.
The stars angels without wings be ever with us as we gain these things.
These are not needed as you see, because these beings that be have a way to be of flight of unseen ways.
They are as solid as you and me and do not fly in a ghostly film.
We do not do astral as we travel, for there are ships to take us there.
So remember, as we go our busy ways, to listen and to see within. Yes, you, and you, and me.
Love eternal we shall always be.

As Grace finished speaking, she introduced me to everyone and asked me to come up and give a short talk. So I went up and gave a talk with the message from Lobe. Afterwards, there was not a sound in the chapel, for all of them were wiping their eyes with the news of the message. They all received their own personal messages. I then sat down. We sang a song, but only one verse was sung.

What Glorious Scenes Mine Eyes Behold
What glorious scenes mine eyes behold! What wonders
Burst upon my view! When Ephraim's records
I unfold, all things appear divinely
New. All things appear divinely new.

After the song was sung with the organ playing, everyone got up and filed out very peacefully, for they were in awe of the words that had been said in this special chapel meeting. They were still stunned while they were outside, and all they could do was just hug one another, so the moment would be still with them. Each of the ones that had gathered left very quietly and went their own ways.

I left and drove to the farm for the pot luck. When I got there, tables were set up for everyone outside, and all the food was put on one large table according to what is eaten first. We filled our plates with the wonderful array of foods to choose from. We didn't take dessert just yet, because there was too much on our plates. We sat down, put our plates on the table, then got up, held hands and said a blessing for the meal. As we ate, we all began to become alert and into the present, and started talking to one another. After the dessert and the clean-up, we all went home to rest for the remainder of the day.

As I got home and put my truck away, I went inside the cottage and changed into comfortable clothing, then brought Sparkle inside. I went to take a nap.

This time it was someone different who spoke to me, and this was while I was still awake.

"My beloved one, I come to you at this time because I first want you to get used to hearing my voice. It is not time for me to tell you my name, because I am giving you some lessons to learn and meditate on. For now I will come to you, just to say hello, and let you know that I love you. It is time for me to go now, and I will be back again soon. I watch and protect you always."

This time I didn't dream, but had a very nice nap. When I woke up, it was 5:30 PM and I decided to fix a light supper of a green salad, soup and toast, with ice tea and honey. I then fed Sparkle and let her out for a bit, and then brought her back in. I said to her, "This is truly a wonderful Sunday, isn't it? I am going to read for a while and then go to bed, how about you, Sparkle?" And then I realized that my dog couldn't read. That was silly of me. I thought I had better cover the birds for the night.

All of a sudden, there was thunder and lightning and then a strong rain. I said, "Wow. What was that all about?" It was soon over and peaceful again. "Do you know what, Sparkle?"

My dog tilted her head in question.

"I'm going to bed now. How about you?"

Sparkle barked, wagged her tail, and we both went to bed and didn't wake up until morning.

I woke up at 6:00 AM, for some reason, and went downstairs and it was really cold, so I fixed a fire in the fireplace to warm the downstairs, and then went in and made coffee. Soon Sparkle came in, and I put her outside, but noticed there was a foot of snow on the ground. Sparkle went out anyway because she had to go potty. I was glad I had gotten up early, for I had to shovel a path out the door and to the garage, and it was good that I had snow tires put on the other day, for I didn't feel like getting down now and putting chains on all the tires. This was work. I thought I would make oatmeal for breakfast and a hot roll. I had a lot to do today. Maybe I would treat myself to lunch at the diner after I took care of business. So I got dressed. I needed warm clothes today. After some breakfast, I felt nice and warm. "Oh my, I forgot poor Sparkle," so I ran and opened the door in the back to let her in, then said, "My poor baby, here, sit by the fire and I will towel dry you. While I am gone, I will turn the heater on low, so all of you will be warm while I am away, doing my errands. Goodbye now. I love all of you and I will be back before long."

I got into the truck and started out. "Well, good morning, world. It's a nice, sparkling, white winter day today. You are so amazing in all that you do!" Everything was so beautiful as I drove toward the next town. Because our town didn't have a DMV or a Social Security office, I had to drive to the next town. The city I was going to was Klamath Falls, Oregon.

Thank goodness it was early, because when I stopped at the Social Security office, I was able to get right in. I just had some papers to fill out, and that was all. They told me that my first check would go to my bank, and that my Medicare card would arrive in about six weeks or less.

"So thank you, Yahweh, for helping me, and for being with me in spirit."

Next, I went to the DMV and was fortunate there as well, since the line was short. I gave my new address for my registration on my truck, and also filled out some papers to get my address changed on my driver's license. They told me I could still use the one I had until my new one arrived in two weeks.

When I got back in my truck, I said another prayer, and thanked everyone above for their help in getting this all done so fast.

I drove back to Welcome Home. I was officially a new townsperson.I then said, "This calls for a celebration. When I get to the general store, I am buying a steak for Sparkle and one for me, and a special treat for my birds."

First, I stopped at the small post office, to check and see if I had any mail in my P.O. box, and to my delight, I did. Then I wondered how Sparkle was feeling, for being left outside so long. The voice said, "She is going to be just fine, and won't be sick from all of this. She is being watched over, just as you are."

I told my guide, "Thank you, and now I feel better."

Next, I went to the general store to buy a couple of nice steaks and some bird treats for my three birds, as well as some special wine to keep at home, to either drink once in a while or to use for cooking. There was no need for the storekeeper's son to help carry things for me today, for I didn't have that much.

I went to check out Dr. Adam Brooks, the local general practice doctor, to set up an appointment for the following month, to check on my heart. The old-fashioned office had a wooden name tag on the door. I walked in and the nurse greeted me and said her name was Janet. Then she asked, "How can I help you?"

I set up the appointment for next month and told her I was still getting settled in my new home. I told the nurse, "For some reason I have heard of that name — Dr. Adam Brooks — before, but I can't recall where." Then I asked her if they took Medicare, and she said yes. She gave me an appointment card and I left.

I checked with the vet to ask about my dog, and wondered when I could bring her in for a checkup. He said, "Anytime you want." The vet's name was Skip, and I thought it fitting, being he took care of animals.

I was hungry, so I stopped at the diner before going home and ordered another veggie burger and everything that went with it. After I ate my lunch, I paid and left a tip, then drove home.

I took my mail and food items inside, then put my truck in the garage. Then I went inside and took my jacket off, hung it up, and sat in my rocker to read my mail. I had to get up to let Sparkle out, then let her back in, for it was cold. I decided to make a fire again in the fireplace so that I could turn off the heater. I put on warm slippers and finally sat down and read my mail.

Thank goodness there were no bills from my other house in California. I did have a letter from my old job and one from my parents. First, I opened the letter from my boss at the bookstore. She told me everything was going well and that they all missed me very much. She was lucky to find a replacement right away. She said, "Anytime you come down this way for a visit, please drop by and say hello. Love and hugs, Mandy."

Then I opened my parents' letter, and they said that they would be coming up for visit on Father's Day weekend. They wrote, "We have a surprise to tell you, but you must wait until June all right. This is short, for we are busy with our upcoming project. So much love is sent to you, my dear. Love, Mom and Dad."

Then there was a letter from my son and his wife and my daughter and her husband, and they all, too, were coming up for a visit on Father's Day weekend. I was so delighted by this news, I wanted to jump for joy. You see, I had gotten married as soon as I'd gotten out of high school, and been married until I turned 50, at which time my husband Mike got real sick and had to have tests made. It turned out to be cancer. He only lived a year after that, because the cancer was so widespread. Before my husband died, he had said to me something at that time I did not understand. "I still have work to do on the other side. I will be waiting for you with open arms."

So yes, I am a widow. This news about my family and my two children coming in June was a wonderful surprise. I knew I had a lot to do before they came for a visit.

Before I got busy doing things that needed doing, I just sat there and daydreamed and said a prayer of thanks for all that Yahweh and Yeshua do for me every day. Then I got up and decided to do something creative for my father. This would be a wood frame to put a special letter in from me to him as a keepsake.

Suddenly, I realized I'd forgotten to put the food away, so I took care of this next. I gave the birds their treats and started cleaning my cottage. I also did a wash. I couldn't hang my wash out because it would freeze solid, so I had to put everything in the dryer. When I was done with that, I put everything upstairs and took a nap. I wondered if there was room in the attic for my family when they came to visit. After my nap I would look and see. I didn't look at the attic after all, for I got busy with something else. It took me a while to get to sleep, because I was excited about the letters from my family and former boss Mandy. But finally I did nod off and had a daytime dream again.

This time I was riding a horse. Her name was Ginger because of her coat, which was almost a reddish color. As we were enjoying our ride we came upon a meadow and stopped. We didn't move because in the meadow were some baby brown bears playing and having a wonderful time. I scanned the area for the mother, because I didn't want to have her attack us. Then I saw her. She was in the tall grass, resting while her cubs played. I moved away and continued my pleasant ride.

Next we came to a river that had a small rapids and I stopped so that Ginger could get a drink. I got off my horse to relax for a bit. I saw a golden object in the water and it looked old. I kneeled down and picked it up, and the writing on it was unknown to me. It was a small pendant, with a pyramid in the middle of it. There was an amethyst below the sun, and in the center of the sun was a sunstone. At the right was a moon with a moonstone in the center of it. At the bottom left and right, were two more gemstones: one a ruby and one a blue sapphire.

Then I heard a voice say to me, "You will need to place this in a special place in your room, for this is an object of where you are from. You are not to wear this pendant just now, because the time is not right. You will find this pendant when you are awake."

Then I woke up and realized it was 5:00 PM and I needed to fix supper. I washed a potato, put it in the oven, made a salad and recalled that I had the last piece of pie in the refrigerator for after supper, and that would be my dessert. The wine was chilling on its side, so I waited until about ten minutes before my baked potato was done cooking. Then I put my two steaks in the broiler for five minutes on each side. Then it was time to eat.

I cut Sparkle's steak for her after it cooled a little, and then gave it to her. She was in heaven with her steak and gobbled it up fast. I said, "Be careful girl." But she was only interested in eating. I said a blessing and ate my supper too. Then she came up to me and licked my cheek in her way of saying thank you, and then rolled on her back for me to rub her tummy. Next she went over to the fireplace and curled up with a smile and rested for a while.

After supper, I took my pie and wine into the living room, and ate my pie and drank my small glass of wine. I enjoyed the rest of the evening before going up to bed for the night. After a while I got up and said, "Sparkle, I am going to bed. How about you?" I first let her outside one more time to do her business. Soon she came back inside and we both went upstairs to bed. We had had a busy day.

I must have really been tired that night, because it was 8:00 in the morning when I got up. I needed to let the dog outside. After I did this, I ran upstairs and got dressed, because I had a lot to do before going to the beauty shop. Then I let the dog inside and fed her, and warmed some coffee in the microwave and just had cold cereal for breakfast. Next I fed my birds. I went back upstairs and made my bed, then washed my face, for I was still a little groggy. Maybe everything had all come down on me and I had done way too much in the last few weeks. I was thinking that maybe I was just plain tired and worn out. Who knows? I said to myself, "I just need to take it a little slower because there is no rush any more and it is winter now, after all. Today is my day just to relax and be pampered, because I deserve it."

I did a little bit of housework, then turned the heater on low. I started the fireplace and made sure Sparkle had plenty of water until I came home. I gave the dog a hug and left. After that, I drove the truck out of the garage. As I rolled into town, I was starting to feel a little more awake and was looking forward to my pampering at the beauty shop.

When I went inside, Pat was there still working on another lady. She said, "Have some coffee and a donut. I am almost done here." I hung my jacket on the coat rack, then helped myself to some coffee and a raised donut, then sat down and thumbed through a magazine while waiting my turn.

There was another lady waiting for the other beautician, whose name was Linda, and we talked for a bit. She was telling me about a tea party she went to not long ago and how much fun it was. Her name was Nancy. "This is nice," I was thinking, for I was finally able to fully relax and get to know the townspeople, and that tea party sounded like fun.

I asked her if she was going to another tea party, and Nancy said, "Next month sometime. Would you like to go with me? We can bring a guest."

I said I would love that. Nancy said, "It's a Valentine's Day theme. Each tea party has a special theme."

I said, "Well, that does sound like fun. Here is my phone number. Why don't you call me later, to let me know what all I need to wear, and so on, okay?"

Nancy said, "Of course."

Pat called my name and I was escorted to a chair to have my hair washed. Afterwards she wrapped a towel around my head, and I sat in her chair so she could do my hair. Pat asked what I wanted done today, and I said that I wanted my hair to go lighter, maybe blond.

Pat said, "That would be nice, of course, but you would look better with some red tones in your hair."

I nodded in agreement and she began to color my hair. As I waited for the color to take effect, one of the ladies asked if I would like a pedicure. I said, "Yes," because I had never had one before. You will never know until you have had one how great this feels. It made my feet really feel good.

Soon my hair was ready to check, and with my pedicure done, I walked over and sat in Pat's chair again. She said the color was just right, and took me to rinse my hair and put a conditioner on it, so my hair would not be so dry. She patted my hair dry and then started to place curlers in my hair. When she was done with this, she put me under the dryer.

Then another lady came and smiled, sat down, and did my nails. My mind kind of drifted for a little while because this was the first time I had ever taken the time to do something just for me, and this felt wonderful. Soon my hair was ready for Pat to take out the curlers, and I walked to her chair again. She took out the curlers and started to comb my hair.

When she was done with my hair and handed me the mirror, I was truly pleased. I thanked her and told her how much I enjoyed her beauty shop. I told her, "I will be back the day before the tea party, to get a touch-up and facial next time." I then gave her a nice tip for a great job, after paying for all that was done. Then I left, feeling brand new and happy.

I spotted a dress store named *Sally's Lace*. I went inside and was in awe at how colorfully she arranged all the dresses. Sally came up to me and asked if I needed any help. I said, "Yes. I have to find a nice outfit for the tea party, and a hat and gloves. I want to look like a lady with style." I smiled to myself for saying such a thing as that, and laughed too, and so did Sally.

We had fun choosing what I should wear, and I think I found another friend. After I was done deciding and trying on dresses, I found the perfect one that had a Victorian look to it. It was just perfect for the tea party. I thanked her for her help and she put my new outfit in a special garment bag, so it would not get wrinkled on the way home. The hat and gloves went into a special hat box. Then I paid for my purchases and left.

By now I was hungry again, so I went to the diner and had a special tuna salad on pita bread with fresh fruit and an herbal iced tea. After I ate, I paid the cashier and went home. As I was driving home I had so many good feelings and thoughts about the new life I had, and it was all good.

Just before I left town, I stopped at the post office to check my mail, and saw that I had a lot of mail today. I had a lot of catalogs and junk mail too. But that's okay, for life was starting to get back to normal. Then I headed home, and when I got home, Sparkle was so glad to see me, her tail was wagging a mile a minute. I hugged her and gave her tummy a good rub, then put my truck in the garage.

When I was back inside, I turned off the heater and made a fire in the fireplace. For some reason I felt like writing a letter to Mom and Dad, and to my son and daughter, as well as Mandy, so after this was done I went in the kitchen and put on a tea kettle of water for herb tea and then sat at the kitchen table for a while and looked through all the mail I had.

Sparkle wanted out, so I put her out in the yard for a while to play, even though there was snow on the ground. I went back to my mail and put the junk mail in the trash for recycles. I looked through the catalogs to see what was new, and then there was a special letter from a long-lost friend.

Before I started to read the letter, the tea kettle started to tweet because it was in the shape of a bird. I poured the water in my tea cup which was made for tea, and poured some honey into it.

Just as I was about to read my letter, the phone rang. It was Nancy calling me. She said she called to tell me all of the details about the tea party, and I must have read her mind, for she told me what type of outfit they had in mind for the party.

I said, "You know what?"

She said, "What is it, Mary?"

"I went to the dress store after leaving the beauty shop and bought an outfit like you just mentioned, and it's a peach color with flowers on the print of the dress, with a matching hat and gloves and even shoes in plain peach color."

She said, "Oh my, that is just perfect. I can hardly wait to see what you look like when I come to pick you up on Valentine's Day."

I asked, "Can we bring a hostess gift?"

She said, "Yes, for each month we have it at a different house. But it is something that one would use for a tea party."

I said, "Thank you for all of this information. We said our goodbyes and hung up the phone. Wow, this was going to be a lot of fun.

By now Sparkle wanted in, so I opened the back door and let her in. I forgot about my letter, so saved it until after supper that night. I drank my now cold tea and took the tea bag out of the cup and said, "I can warm that up later this evening before I go to bed." It was 5:00 now, and I started to get supper ready. I fed Sparkle and myself, then cleaned up and decided to warm up my tea.

I did so, and took my tea and sat in the living room by the fire. Finally I read my letter. It was from Anita, and she had contacted my Mom and Dad, since they still lived where they knew one another since high school. They had given her my new address. I was so happy to hear from her, because we had been good friends in school. In the letter she asked, "Could I come visit you sometime? I want to regain our friendship. I am divorced now and need to talk to someone. You were always a comfort to me when I was feeling low. Would it be all right to visit you on your birthday?" Then she said that she never had any children, only a pet dog named Max. He was a Golden Lab. She said, "When I come, may I bring him? That's it for now, and when you have a chance, please write back. Love and hugs, Anita."

For some reason it came to me that she was reaching out because of something else other than being lonely. Perhaps she desperately needed my help and advice.

It was time for bed, so I covered my birds for the night and turned off the lights, then went up to bed with Sparkle at my heels. I was very tired, so after getting ready for bed, I went to sleep right away. Then I heard a voice say, "Your friend is very sick, and she will tell you about it when she sees you on your birthday."

When I got up the next morning, I noticed it was snowing again. I let the dog out anyway, and it was cute to see her jump up to catch the snowflakes in her mouth. Then I said, "This calls for a new fire in the fireplace. I also had better call and get another cord of wood today."

I let Sparkle in, and she shook the snow off of her fur. It looked like she had a smile on her face, so I got a towel and helped dry her off. She then sat by the fire to get warm while I fixed breakfast. Today called for hot cocoa and that is what I made to drink instead of coffee. Then I fed my dog and cooked my oatmeal and had toast as well. After breakfast, I decided to be a little lazy today and just kick back for a while.

I sat at the kitchen table and wrote a letter to my friend Anita. I wrote, "Dear Anita: I got your letter yesterday and you wanted to know if you could come to see me. Of course you can come and stay awhile. Bring Max, your Lab. I know that Sparkle would love to have a pal to play with. I am still new to this lovely little town, as well as my cottage, and have not really looked around the grounds that much, but I did see an extra little place that just might be a place for a guest. I will check it out this afternoon and then and tell you in another letter what it's like. It was snowing when I got up, so I am being lazy this morning. Well, give me your phone number when you write back, so I can call you. All right? I've got to go now. Love and hugs, Mary."

Then I added: "P.S. I just went outside a while ago and found the mini cottage, and it's a one-floor, one bedroom, and is just right for you. I also found a barn that I am going to tell George about." After writing my letter, I gathered the other three letters that I had forgotten to mail yesterday, and decided to take them to town when the snow lifted up a bit.

I put on my jacket, boots, hat and gloves, and decided to go outside and look around even if it was snowing. Sparkle wanted to go, too, so off we went, exploring my back yard. Then I saw the little building that seemed to me like a guest room, and opened the door. It was a one-bedroom cottage, and when I looked further, I said, "This will be perfect for my friend. But, wow, does it ever need cleaning!" But I could do that tomorrow. This was really a cute place for her, and it was all one floor and made to look just like my cottage, only smaller.

It was a good thing I hadn't sealed the envelope yet, because I wanted to tell Anita what I'd found. So I closed the door and did some more exploring around the yard. Then I came upon a nice barn and went inside. I said, "Wow, this has great possibilities, in case I want to get a horse later and three cows, because I see where there is a place for milking cows. How great is this!" Then I saw an upstairs where hay could be stored. I would have to show George this and see what he thought. I was glad that I decided to not do much of anything that day, but I knew I had better go inside and write to Anita about what I discovered before I sent the letter.

But before that, I decided to put some dry clothes on. So off I went to the cottage, completed Anita's, letter, and then changed my clothes. When I got inside, I helped Sparkle dry off and then I got dry and changed my clothes. Afterwards, I came downstairs and wrote the "P.S." in my letter. Finally, I was ready to go to the post office and mail my four letters.

"Well, Sparkle, would you like to go to town with me?"

From the wagging of her tail and her smile, I already knew the answer to that. Thank goodness, the snow was not staying too heavy on the ground. It was easy to get to the garage, and I opened the back part of my truck and Sparkle jumped inside. Then I got in, and backed out. I got out and shut the door to the garage.

The snow was starting to let up a little, so it was not as hard trying to see the road to town. When I got there, I first went to the post office and mailed my letters and bought more stamps. Then checked my P.O. box and saw that I had a lot of mail again. I took it out and then went and put it in my truck and drove to the library to take my books back.

Grace was there and said, "Good morning. We are looking forward to having you come again this Sunday to the chapel. Would you like to give another talk sometime?"

I said I would have to work on it because I wanted to have a special one for all of them. "How about my giving a talk on Mother's Day? Would that be all right?"

She said, "It's perfect."

I checked out three more books and then left. For some reason, I wanted to talk to George, so I used my cell phone and called him, to see if I could drop by. He answered the phone and I asked him and he said, "Of course. Come on by."

Then I drove with my dog out to his farm. He said, "Come on inside and have some coffee so we can talk, and bring your dog inside with you."

The two of us went to the farmhouse. I wiped off my dog's feet and went inside. We all sat down and talked, and I told George about the barn that I discovered that morning.

George said that he already knew about the barn. He said, "Many years ago the lady who was living there did have a horse and three cows, and there is a milking machine as well, but you may have to have it checked out, to make sure it's working properly." Then he said, "I know a dairy farmer not far from here that when you decide to buy some cows, he will help you with instructions on how to take care of cows, and how to use the milking machine. There are a lot of farmers around here that can give you advice on almost anything you need to know."

I said, "Thank you so much for helping me with this. This has been very enlightening for me. Well, I have to go now, and do two more errands and then go home." We said goodbye and I left.

I was on my way into town when I saw the sun peeking through the clouds and knew it might warm up, but even with this little break I knew that winter was not nearly finished yet. I decided to stop at the bakery and get some fresh bread and some cinnamon rolls for breakfast tomorrow. After doing that, I went to the hardware store to get some tools for working on the mini cottage, and then went home.

After I got home and put everything away, I made a fire in the fireplace and then said, "Oh dear, I forgot to order some more wood." So I went to the phone and called and asked them to bring a cord of wood to my cottage. Within an hour they came and delivered it, and I paid for it, and then they left.

Then I read my mail. There was another letter from my parents, before I had a chance to mail theirs. That was okay, because I loved to get letters. It was from Mom, and she said she already sent me a letter a few days ago, but wanted to have me check some things out for her. "Could you please see if they have any places in your town for sale, for we would like to check on this for someone?"

I gave Mom a call on the telephone and she was glad to hear from me so fast. I said, "This won't take up your time, but here is the phone number of a Realtor in town you can talk to, and let me know what I can do to help, all right?" We said goodbye to one another and I gave her my love.

After I hung up the phone, my mind was working overtime. I said to myself: "Something is going on here, and I wonder what they are cooking up."

Then I decided to check out the attic, to see what shape it was in. I pulled the attic steps down and took my flashlight and climbed up and looked around. This was perfect for an extra room for guests, and to my surprise, it already had been worked on, for just that purpose. All it needed was some dusting and cleaning and fresh linens put on the beds. There were two bedrooms up there. This was perfect for my family. I wondered why there were stairs on the back side of the house, and now I knew. "Thank you, Yahweh. This cottage is truly magical, as I felt it was."

I then went back down and knew I had a lot of work ahead of me. It was fun work. I made a list to buy new sheets and towels, for I didn't have enough for everyone to use. Also I would need extra dishes and flatware. It's a good thing my dining room table had three extensions in the closet and I had two extra chairs.

I was getting very excited about this visit in June. Well, first things first. I needed to get the mini cottage cleaned for March. One thing for sure, I was not ever bored, was I?

The next morning, when I woke up, to my surprise the sun was shining. This was wonderful. I looked out the window, and even all the snow had melted. I put on my robe and slippers and went downstairs with Sparkle at my heels. I let her out the back door, then went to the kitchen to make a pot of coffee. My, how good the coffee smelled as I opened the container to scoop it out.

Next, I went into the bathroom. When I came out, I was refreshed for the morning. I let Sparkle back in and fed her. It felt a little chilly still, so I turned on the heater for a little while, then went to the sun room and uncovered my birds and changed their water and fed them. They tweeted with joy at the sight of the sun, and my mynah bird just whistled.

Now I was ready to make a nice breakfast, because for some reason I felt extra hungry this fine morning. After breakfast and the cleanup, I went upstairs and got dressed in some old clothes, then came downstairs and gathered my cleaning supplies and went out the back door.

I went into the mini cottage and opened all the windows. Some were stuck, so I had a little prying to do in order to have fresh air. I took all the curtains down and gathered the linens in the cottage and put them in a pile on the floor. I took them to the wash room and placed them in the washer with soap, then turned the machine on. Then I went back to the cottage and did a complete cleaning, which only took about three hours. Next, I gathered all my things and returned to my place and put them away.

The linens were now ready for the dryer, so I placed them in to dry. It was almost time for lunch, so I went out to the mini cottage first and closed all the windows, then came back in. For some reason, I made a mental note to get new curtains and other things I needed later, and wrote it all down, then sat down at the kitchen table for a minute or so.

I got up, made a sandwich, and had some juice to drink. The phone rang. It was George. He called to ask if he could come over later with his friend from the dairy farm, to look at my barn. I said, "Sure, that would be fine."

It was still early, so I sat in the living room and folded the linens I brought in from the washroom, and then put them away. I put the ones that needed to be ironed into a nice covered basket for later, and then just relaxed for a while. I browsed through my catalogs to see what was new.

Soon there was a knock on my door, and I got up to answer it. It was George and the man from dairy farm named Sam. They came in and we talked a minute, and then we walked out to the barn. They looked around and asked if I would mind if they took the milking machines with them when they left, as well as the other equipment that went along with it.

"We will be sending a crew out here to clean up the barn for you, to get it ready for spring."

I said, "Sure, if that's all right with everyone."

They said, "Yes, we are a community of people that take care of our own. And we all work together. Also, we want to donate three cows this spring, so you have a start, and we heard that you like goat's milk. Would it be all right to also build a special place for goats? This is one thing we don't have in our area — a goat milk dairy. And we will repair all of the fences, so they don't get loose."

Then I said, "It's so nice of all of you." I had tears in my eyes. I told them about my friend coming to visit on my birthday on St. Patrick's Day, and that she would be staying with me because she was all alone.

They said, "If you need any help, just let us all know." Then they left.

For some reason, I had to kneel down right where I was at, and say a thank you to Yahweh for sending these wonderful people over, to offer me such loving help.

A voice said to me, "My child, this is Yahweh. You are loved more than you know for all of your good works."

Then the tears really came down, because I felt all this pure love coming from the heavenly father to me like a big hug. All I could do now as I went inside was just sit and relax and savor what I had experienced. For some reason I was not even hungry.

Sparkle put her head in my lap and looked into my eyes, then licked my cheeks. She knew how I felt and was there for me. Yes, animals are our true friends when we are feeling low and also when we are happy. And yes, they have souls. They are our guides, too.

After this, I did get something to eat, and I fed Sparkle and covered my birds for the night before I went up to bed.

The experience would stay with me for a long time. I had a little trouble getting to sleep, so I said a prayer to help me and then I was in a deep sleep.

In the early morning hours I had another dream. In this one I saw a beautiful, clear blue sky with a few clouds that looked like little sheep hopping about, and on the ground was a valley of tall grass and wild flowers, and a mountain in the distance with snow at the top of it. There was a winding stream going through this valley. It gave me a very calming feeling.

When I woke up, I felt wonderful on this brand new day, and I did what I normally did every morning, then got dressed and put a leash on Sparkle and hook her for a short walkl. The sun was out again and the ground was dry. We walked in another direction this time.

When we came to a bridge, it was strange because it was a bridge made out of rope and below it was the rapids. Then I said, "Do you want to try walking on the bridge?" She answered by wagging her tail, so we started to walk on this bridge. It swayed a bit, but that was all right.

When we got to the middle of the bridge, we stopped and looked down. What we saw was the churning of water that gave off the color of light aqua blue, with the foam of the strong current of the river below. It was breath-taking to see the way of nature and what she does. As we walked across this bridge it led into a bunch of thick, tall trees, and the sun was blocked out for a little while, because these trees were so tall.

I think they might have been a small grove of redwoods. They had the feel of a cathedral, only natural, and you could also sense how quiet it was. You could *feel* the quiet. You knew this place was indeed a place to come to again, to be alone and to be at peace.

We then turned around and went back home, and I decided to go to town because I had not picked up my mail in a couple days. So I grabbed my purse and put Sparkle in the yard with fresh water until I came home, then got my truck out of the garage, got in and backed out. Then I got out again and closed the garage door and drove to town. It was still too cool to use my golf cart.

I went to the post office first, and yes, I did have a lot of mail, so much that if I hadn't had my shopping bags with me, I could not have carried it all.

My next stop was at a different store. This was a health food store. I parked my truck and got out, then noticed the store was close to everything, so I could leave my truck here and go anywhere I wished. I walked inside the health store and looked around. There was so much to see. A young woman came up to me to ask if I needed any help, and I said, "Yes, could you please help me find some good organic flour and other things I can use to bake with?"

I then saw some aloe-vera gel, so I picked up a bottle of this and then some other organic things I wanted. Then I saw a juice bar and had a glass of carrot juice. It was very good. The young woman's name was Lisa. Soon I had everything I needed and went to the cashier and paid for them and left. I went to the yardage store, which was a few buildings away. I was just looking today, but wanted to see what they had for a future project I was thinking about making. When I was done looking, I left.

Next I noticed a small tea house, so I went inside and took a seat where the lady directed me. I sat down at this cute table and read the menu. The lady was named Geneva. I ordered tea and the special treats to go with it. This was a very nice place to come, where you didn't want anything heavy to eat. When what I ordered came to the table, I was in awe of how pretty everything was arranged, so I just enjoyed this for a while, and then paid for everything I had at the table. This was very elegant, and a special place. I wanted to savor every moment.

Afterwards I left and drove home, then said to myself, "There is so much to explore. It is mind-boggling." When I returned home and parked my truck, I had to make two trips to carry what I had into my cottage. Then I left my truck out because I felt like I may have to use it again that day.

Before I got relaxed, I let my dog in, then sat down and went through my pile of mail. I had several letters as well. Mom and Dad's, and my son's and daughter's, and my friend's. I took my personal letters in the living room, where I felt like making a fire in the fireplace.

After doing this, I sat down in my comfortable chair and read all my mail. I read my parents' letter first, because I felt it was important. Ye, lo and behold, it was, when I started reading it. They said, "We are so sorry to keep you in all of this suspense of what we are doing. So we decided to tell you what we are planning. The reason we needed a Realtor is this: We are going to buy a home in your town, and we may also be coming for the Mother's Day weekend, so we can look at some places. This was the surprise, so we will be coming in May and also June."

When I read this, I wanted to jump for joy because then I would have my parents close by when they moved here. Next, I opened my son's letter. He, too, said he and his wife would be coming in May because they had some special news for me, and the same went for my daughter's letter.

Well, this was really exciting for me. This meant I had better stock up now, so I would be able to have enough food for everyone.

Then I opened my friend's letter. She asked if she could come sooner than March, because she could not wait any longer to talk to me. She asked if I had the cottage ready, and wanted to move in because she needed to be near someone close. After I read her letter, I called her right away, and asked, "Please tell me now, what is it? Because I am concerned about you."

Then she started to cry and said, "Mary, I am very sick, and don't have very long to live. I wanted to stay with my best friend, so I don't feel so alone. I have leukemia and it's widespread. My doctor said there is nothing else they can do for me."

I then told her, "Oh, my..." I, too, began to cry, and said, "How soon can you get here, and what will you be bringing with you?"

She said, "In three weeks, because I have loose ends to take care of."

"Do you want me to ask the doctor here in town if he can see you and help you through this?" I asked.

She then said, "Yes, please ask him."

I then asked her if she would mind me saying a prayer with her before I hung up the phone.

She said, "Oh Mary, please do, because I really need this."

We said a prayer together and asked Yahweh to help Anita in her hour of need, then thanked him. When we said our goodbyes, I was still in tears as I hung up the phone.

Then I called the doctor and told him about my friend coming to stay with me, and would it be all right for him to come and look after her from time to time?

He said, "Of course, my dear, and we can arrange a nurse to come in and give her medication when she needs it."

Then I said goodbye and thanked him for his help. I knew I would have a nice, fresh-looking cottage for her to move into, with everything bright and inviting. For some reason, I had to call Grace, and tell her about my friend, and she said the ladies of the church would help out too.

"And when she arrives in town, have her come to chapel on the first Sunday she gets here, for it will help her feel better having new friends."

I said, "Thank you so much. I want her last months to be happy ones."

We, too, had a prayer on the phone, for she knew I needed courage to help my friend. I then said goodbye and hung up.

This was a day of new possibilities and challenges for me, with what was coming into my new life. But after all, isn't it what we are all supposed to be doing for one another?

Then I heard another voice answer my question, saying, "Yes, my child, this is all included in your earth plan."

Then I knew that my path had many avenues.

CHAPTER 2

ELL, THIS WAS TOP priority. The mini cottage needed to be fixed up within three weeks. The ladies came the next Monday, bright and early, and we all worked together, painting and putting up new curtains, and installing new carpet. We made sure there was an emergency button on the telephone, to contact the doctor in case he was needed.

There was a kitchenette for my friend and a small bathroom with a shower and new towels, and fresh new linens on the bed. Finally, the mini cottage was ready for my friend and an extra garage was built onto mine for her car.

The big day arrived. On Thursday afternoon Anita drove onto my property. I went to meet her with open arms. With Yahweh's blessing, the sun was shining this first week of February. This was very good because I wanted Anita to have a nice new day and new life for the few months she had left. I ran to the car and helped her out and we gave each other a big hug.

I asked how she had been and she said everything went very nicely. I said, "Come in and rest for a bit, before I take you to your cottage. Someone is coming by soon to help with the unloading and to get you settled in. But, in the meantime, how about some herb tea while we wait and talk? Let's put Sparkle and Max in the back yard, so they can get to know each other, okay?"

Then I put our two dogs in the fenced yard with extra water for them to drink. I came back and got the tea and some treats to eat, since it was mid-afternoon when she arrived.

Anita then told me what the doctors found and all of the chemo she had endured recently. She showed me the medicines she had to take and told me the only family she'd had left was gone now, and that is why she decided to ask if it was all right to come and stay with me. She just did not want to be alone for what time she had left. One never knows when this will happen, for it's in God's hands.

I asked if she had made arrangements for the time this would happen. "I know this is hard for you, but I have to ask these things."

Anita said, "Not yet, but that's another reason I am here, so you can help me through these preparations."

I said, "Of course. That's what friends are for."

Then she said, "When the time comes for me to go home, could you please take care of Max for me? For now he has someone to play with, and it won't be so hard on him when I leave this earth."

I said, "Sure I will, for Sparkle needs a playmate too. This is good. We are able to talk about this now. Then we will have these little things taken care of. There will be some people from the chapel coming by from time to time, to look after you when I go to town. On Valentine's Day I was invited to a tea party. Would you be up to going with us?"

"No, I would really like to stay home and just rest, if you don't mind, dear friend."

"I do understand, and I will leave a phone number, in case you need me when I go to the party."

Then there was a knock on the door, and some of the ladies were here to move Anita's belongings into the mini cottage. While they were taking care of this, we had some more tea, and then one of the ladies came and told me everything was ready and asked for the key to put Anita's car in the garage.

After they did this, they came and greeted my friend and gave her a hug and said they had left their names and phone numbers on her desk. This way Anita could call them while I was out on an errand. They said goodbye and that they were happy to have her join our little town, and then they left.

Anita said she was very tired from her trip and wanted to go lie down and rest, so I took her out there in her wheelchair. She didn't have the strength to walk any farther. I got her settled in and helped her to bed. Before this, she saw what her new home looked like and was very pleased.

Then I said, "Here is an intercom, so you can let me know if there is anything you need. The dogs will be fine now, and when it starts to get dark, I will bring Max over here for you. Have a nice rest, and I will bring you some supper, if you feel like eating. Just let me know, all right?" I left her to rest, and came back and did a few things before starting to fix supper. I, too, rested for a while

Because I was worried about my friend, as I dozed off for a nap, a voice said, "You are a strong woman, and you need to stay strong for her. A place is being prepared for her on the home side, because she is needed here. She is well loved. This is a good thing you are doing for her, and she loves you for it. So rest now and know that I am here for you, my child."

I said, "Thank you, Yahweh, and thank you for your advice and your help." Then I was out like a light and didn't wake up until later.

All of a sudden, I jerked awake. "Oh my gosh! I had better bring the dogs in and take Max over to Anita's. Here Max. Let's go over to your mama now." He followed me to the cottage.

I knocked on Anita's door and she said, "Come in." I brought Max in from being outside.

"And I will feed him while I am here. How are you? Did you have enough rest?"

She said, "Yes. Thank you so much, for I was very comfortable in my new bed."

I asked, "Are you hungry?"

She said, "Do you have any soup, for I just feel like having soup and toast for now, and some more of that herb tea."

"Sure. Is there any kind you prefer?"

"Vegetable beef soup, if you have any."

"Yes, I do. And how about tapioca pudding?"

"Oh yes. I have not had that in years."

"So soup it is. I will be back soon."

I went over and heated up the soup and made some toast and put a dish of pudding on a tray. I walked to the small table and placed her supper on the table with a place mat and napkin. I had a small vase with a flower in it for her.

We talked a while, so she would have company while she was eating. Then I said, "I need to get back and see to Sparkle and feed her and get a bite of food before I turn in. Are you going to be warm enough?"

She said, "I am fine now."

So I gathered up the dishes and came back to my place. I had something to eat as well, after feeding my dog. Then I cleaned up everything and went upstairs after covering the birds.

All of a sudden, I heard thunder and lightning, and then a nice steady rain. I used the intercom and asked Anita if the storm bothered her. She said no, she loved it, so then I said, "Good night now, and have a nice rest." I then turned off the light in my room and went to bed.

The next morning the rain had stopped and the sun was out. I said, "I do think that winter is almost over." I took a shower and dressed, then went downstairs and let my dog out. I saw that Max was at the gate, so I let him in the yard for a little bit. I brought both dogs in and fed them. I had the fireplace going, so they went and got warm and rested together. Next, I uncovered my birds and fed them too.

It was now time to fix breakfast, so I put on a fresh pot of coffee and made a pot of oatmeal, then cut up some fruit and put some in a small bowl. I fixed a tray for my friend and took it over to her.

Anita was up and dressed and looked like she was rested from her long drive. I told her I had some errands to run and asked if she would be okay while I was gone.

She said she would be fine and might sit outside in the sun and enjoy the view, then later go in and read.

"That's good. I will see about getting a P.O. box for you. Do you have a change of address card filled out already?"

She said, "Yes."

"I will take your card with me. And when I get to the post office, I will put your box number on the card. This way your mail can start coming to you. Goodbye now, and enjoy your day, and I will pick up the dishes on my return. I may bring home a hamburger for us. It may be junk food, but, heck, we don't eat that every day."

She said, "I would love that."

Then I left and was on my way, but I put the dogs out before I left. While in town, I went to the general store and bought a lot of food this time, so there would be a variety to choose from for our meals. This time I let Steve bring it all to my truck. I had an ice chest for the cold items with ice in it, then went to the hardware store and got some things I needed from Hank.

Hank asked, "How is your friend doing?"

I said, "She is better after resting from her long trip."

He said, "That's very good to hear."

I then said goodbye and went to the library to take my books back. I didn't get any other books today because I told Grace I had to get back. She understood, and I was on my way to the post office.

I rented a box for Anita and then put the number of the box on the change-of-address card, picked up my own mail, and had two more stops before I went home. One was the bakery, and then I went to the diner. I got two hamburgers with fries and root beer for each of us. The items were packed so as they would not spill. I put this on the floor on the passenger's side of my truck.

Then I said, "I need to get some treats for the pets," so I went to the pet store and bought a bunch of them. I was finally on my way home.

By the time I got home, I was starved, so I quickly put away everything and left the truck outside, then went to Anita's cottage and we ate our lunch together. Afterwards, I took the tray and picked up the breakfast dishes and went to my own cottage, put away my truck, and came back to relax awhile.

I really had a lot of mail again, so I sat at my kitchen table and went through it as always. I had another letter from my parents and also from my son and daughter, and from Mandy, the boss at the bookstore I used to work for. I started to read all of my mail, one letter at a time. I felt good while I opened my Mom's letter. It read:

Dear Mary:

We have great news for you. We found a nice place not far from you. We will be next door almost. It's a small farm where we can raise horses because this has been our dream since we first were married. It's the old Wallace farm and has a very up-to-date stable and corral for horses on seven acres. The fences have been replaced with new ones. Anyway, we were able to sell our home for the full price and will be moving at the end of February, so you don't have to make room for us, because we have a place to stay now, and it's our own. We will call you before we move, to let you know when we are coming, and don't worry, for we have taken care of everything. How is Anita doing? We pray for her every day and send our love. Well, just wanted you to know the good news, so goodbye now.

Love
Mom and Dad

The letter from my son read:

Dear Mom:

We have good news for you. It was supposed to be a surprise, but we could not keep a secret anymore. We, too, have found a place in your town and it's the other direction of your town. It's three acres of land with a nice farm house. We wanted to have a nice size home to raise our children. Our dream, too, has been to grow corn and wheat, so this nice place has the equipment for harvesting of the wheat and the corn. We, too, are moving at the end of February, and everything is taken care of. One last thing we had to tell you, Mom: We are finally going to have a baby, in fact twins, so soon you will be a grandma. How about that? We've got to go, Mom, for we have a lot to do before we move.

Love and hugs
David and Susan

Then I read the letter from my daughter:

Hi, Mom, this is Daisy and Dan:

You have heard that we are all moving at the end of February, and we, too, have bought a farm, because this was Dan's dream as well. It's not far from David and Susan and it's also three acres. We have wanted to have an apple orchard and cherry and peach orchard, so this farm already has the trees, and yes, Mom, I am pregnant and also will be having twins. Isn't this neat? So see you soon. Our babies will be born in September, the same time as David and Susan, so you will have four grandchildren, isn't this exciting? We've got to go and we have a lot of packing to do. See you soon, Mom.

Love and hugs
Daisy and Dan

The last letter was from Mandy, my old boss:

Dear Mary:

This is a beautiful day, isn't it? I just wanted to tell you that I am getting married on June 7, and my wedding will be in your town. The church will be the chapel on the hill you have told me about. I want you to me my maid of honor, please. Also, the lady who owns the bookstore is moving that lives in your town, because she is getting married and does not want to work any more. I remember you telling me about her nice bookstore, and it's just what I wanted. I called her to introduce myself, because you told me how nice she was, and, yes, she is very nice, and she will tell you when she is getting married when you go to town again. Everything is finally falling into place, and please let me know soon, so I can make plans for my wedding. Ever since you told me about your nice town, I knew that I had to move there. My husband-to-be is Stanley and he is going to be working with the vet in your town. I am so excited about all of this. Our dreams are finally coming true. Stanley is a specialist of cattle and horses, so he will be a great asset in your town. I've got to go, but will give you more details in June.

Love and hugs,
Mandy

As I put all the letters down I was stunned with so much good news in one day, and somewhat numb, so I just sat there and looked into the fire so I could pull myself together. For some reason I felt like I needed to take a walk to clear my head. I called Anita and said I was going for a walk and hoped she would be all right until I got back. She said she would be just fine.

I grabbed my jacket and put on my boots and was on my way. As I walked I had all of these thoughts in my head because everything was happening so fast, but I knew that it was going to be wonderful to have all my loved ones with me in the small town, as well as my friend Mandy. Then I knew that when Anita passes on I would have the comfort of my family to be with me.

I came to the rope bridge I had seen the other day, and for some reason it was calling me. As I crossed the bridge, I knew I had to walk farther than the woods on the other side because my guides wanted me to see something, so I did, and then came to another cave. I did not feel unsafe because I knew I was being watched over. Thank goodness this time I had brought a flashlight, because I needed it.

Walking a ways inside, there was a tunnel that was lit up like a new day. Then I felt I didn't need the flashlight anymore. I followed the tunnel and then it opened up to a large area, and in the center of this large area stood a crystal pyramid in pure lavender color. I reached out to touch it, but a voice said, "Wait," so I did.

All of a sudden, a door opened up in the pyramid and out came seven little beings that said to me, "We want you to be the guardian of this cave by putting a blessing on it, so no one comes near. Can you do this for us?"

I said, "Yes. May I ask where you are from?"

They said, "It is not time for you to know right now, because this is for your safety as well as ours." Then they handed me a heart-shaped crystal in dark purple.

I then said, "How do I keep others from coming to this cave?"

They said, "With the crystal. You can slide a boulder over the opening, and each time we call you telepathically, you have the crystal to open the cave."

I then said goodbye to these little beings and left to go home. Somehow I felt better now and uplifted in a big way. This indeed was a close encounter, and I felt these beings needed to be protected from the outside world.

As I left I did as they asked and put the boulder over the opening of the cave. I went back through the woods, crossed the bridge and walked home.

"Wow," I said to myself, "this truly is a wonderful place to live." When I got home, it was starting to get dark, so I brought the dogs inside and fed them, then took Max over to Anita and told her supper would be ready soon.

She said, "Did you have a nice walk?"

I said, "I sure did. Before I start supper, I wanted to ask you... would you like to go to church at the chapel tomorrow? Afterwards they are having pot luck at the farm down the road from there."

She said, "Yes, I would. What time does it start?"

I said, "At nine."

She said, "That's great. I will be ready."

"Okay then. I better get cooking, for I am taking potato salad and a casserole of baked beans and a chocolate cake."

She said, "That is making me hungry. You had better get busy." She laughed. Then she asked, "Could I come and help you? We can eat in your kitchen."

I said, "Of course." Then I was off to fix our small supper.

As I was cooking supper I put some potatoes on to boil and some eggs for the potato salad, then got two cans of baked beans and doctored them up with brown sugar and yellow mustard in a baking dish. I then put them in the refrigerator until morning. Next, I mixed up a chocolate cake and put it in a sheet pan, then put it in the oven to bake. We were having macaroni and cheese with a beet salad for supper, and pudding for dessert.

Anita came in the back door with an apron on, ready to work. First, we ate our supper and had herb tea. After we were done, the cake was ready, so I put it on the sideboard to cool. Then I put marshmallows on top and made a rich frosting with pecans and chocolate and poured it over the top while it was warm. The potatoes were done by now, so I cooled them off, as well as the eggs which I put in cold water. It didn't take long. Then we both peeled them and cut them in small pieces and kept six eggs for deviled eggs.

Then we rinsed our hands and started to dice onions and celery together, because we wanted to get done before it was too late. I mixed up some Miracle Whip and mustard and added some sweet pickle relish. Next, I mixed everything all together and placed it in a large bowl, and put some plastic wrap on top and stuck it in the refrigerator for the night. We fixed the eggs to put on top in the morning. After that was all done, we did up the dishes and Anita went back to her cottage and went to bed.

I let Sparkle out one more time, and then let her in, and we both went upstairs to bed.

The next morning I got up early and took a shower and got dressed. After I let my dog out, I put the beans in the oven to cook, and also placed the eggs on top of the salad and covered it again, then put ice in the ice chest to have it get colder

I brought my dog inside and fed her, made coffee, then called my friend to see if she was ready. We could eat breakfast together. She said she was, and came over and had a coat with her, in case she needed to keep warm. We just had corn flakes and fruit and coffee. Then I put the dogs in the fenced yard with a lot of water and I fed the birds. We next put the salad in the ice chest and the cake in a box, so it would not get messed up, and the beans with a lid on it, into a container to keep them warm.

We then both carried this and put it in the back of the truck. We got in and drove to church.

The chapel was so pretty today. We met Grace and she introduced Anita to everyone, and soon it was time for our service to begin.

Grace got up and gave a beautiful talk and everyone was truly in a loving mood. There were prayers said for Anita for her health, and then we sang only one verse of the hymn:

THE LORD IS MY SHEPHERD

The Lord is my Shep-herd; no want shall I know. I
Feed in green pas-tures; safe-fold-ed I rest. He lead-eth my
Soul where the still wa-ters flow, re-stores me when wan-d'ring,
re-deems when op-pressed, re-stores me when wan-d'ring
re-deems when op-pressed.

I loved that song. Then Grace gave the last thoughts of the morning, and we all greeted one another and hugged. We left for the farm.

When we got there, my friend and I carried the food to the large table with all the other food, but this time they had a different way of doing things. They put each course on three tables. We all joined into a big circle, joined hands, and said the blessing for our food. After this, we all got a paper plate and stood in line for our turn to decide what food we wanted. There was so much food to choose from, it was mind-boggling.

Then we relaxed and had a good time and helped to do cleanup. By then, Anita said she was feeling tired, so I gathered our dishes and put them in the truck and we said our goodbyes and left.

When we got home, Anita went to her cottage and changed clothes and just had to lie down. She was tired. I went upstairs for a nap. Then I got up and let the dogs in, for it was starting to get dark and a little cold. I fed them and took Max to be with my friend for the night.

I asked if she was hungry, and she said, "No. I am still full from the big pot luck." We said our good nights and I went to bed at my place. I was not hungry. I went to asleep right away.

The next morning was a little overcast, and I heard them saying on the news it might rain that day. I got dressed, went downstairs, let Sparkle out and uncovered the birds, then turned on the heater to low. Then I let Sparkle in and fed her.

Next, I fixed breakfast and took a tray over to my friend's cottage, and asked if she was warm enough. I told her I would be going to town to take care of some things and would try not to be too long. I asked, "Do you want me to send the man from the Happy Rest Mortuary to talk to you today? For you mentioned, when you got here, you needed to take care of this."

She said, "Yes, you are right, I can't put this off any longer."

I said, "I will do this for you and also pick up your mail, if you have any."

She thanked me, but before I left, I asked, "If it rains, could you have Sparkle and your Max come inside your place while I am gone?"

She said, "Yes, I can do that."

I then went to my place and put Sparkle outside and I grabbed my jacket and got into my truck and drove to town. As I was driving I looked at the gas gauge and it was a little low, so I stopped in to fill her up. After doing this, I drove to the Happy Rest Mortuary, to speak to Mr. Graves, and asked if he would go to visit Anita at her cottage, and he said he would, so I thanked him and was on my way. Soon I was at the post office and picked up my mail as well as Anita's.

Then I decided to just leave my truck parked and go to the book store. As I walked into the book store, Jill said, "Come back here while I do my work. I have some news for you. I am getting married in May. I am so happy."

My friend had called her and they had become friends. Her wedding was in June.

"This is wonderful," I said. "Are you going to keep on working at this store?"

She said, "No, because I want to become a full-time house wife and have a family."

"What will become of your book store?"

She said, "Mandy bought it. She must have told you."

I said, "Yes, she did, but I wanted to hear your story, because then I could get all the details from you, and besides, I know that you wanted to tell me everything."

She said, "You are right, and I am so glad you came in today, so I could tell you."

I said, "There has been a lot of exciting news going around this week, and this makes me very happy. Jill, I am so very happy for you."

She said, "Thank you so much." She then gave me a big hug.

I left, and stopped in the diner, because I hadn't eaten breakfast yet. As I entered, Cindy came up and gave me a hug for some reason. She said, "I am so glad you moved to our town, and I hope this does not sound strange. I love you, dear, because I feel that I know you from many eons ago."

This seemed surprising that someone from a new town would tell me this. I was shown a table and handed a menu..

I thanked her and said, "When you have a day off, come by and take a walk with me?" She said she would, then went to get my water and coffee.

I was extra hungry by now, so I ordered the special of two eggs and two each of bacon and link sausage, hash browns, and one pancake on the side. As soon as my breakfast arrived, I got busy and ate. I ate all of it. When I was done, I left my tip, paid the cashier, and left.

As I drove home, everything came to me at once. I said, "Yaw-hoo!" out loud.

When I got home, I did the usual. I went inside and said a special prayer for Yahweh, and then I heard his voice say to me, "Child, you are very welcome. All is falling into place for you, for this town you were guided to move to, and you are doing well. Some big work is being planned for you."

I said thank you, and he said, "You are welcome, child."

I then noticed that the mortuary car was still over at Anita's cottage, so I walked over to see if there was anything I could help with. Mr. Graves said that everything was all set now. His first name was Dick.

After he left, I asked my friend how she was feeling and if she was hungry.

She said, "I am not feeling too well and I'm not very hungry."

I said, "Would you like me to call the doctor?"

She said, "Please do. Something is different in how I feel, and I want to know what it is."

As I gathered the breakfast dishes, I was worried deep inside. I went to my place before I started to cry. It was best that I call the doctor. I asked if he could come by and check on my friend. He said he would come right away.

He was there before I knew it. I think he felt what I did. He then gave her a check-up and said, "I better have you check into the hospital today, and I will drive you there now."

So off they went. I said I would be by in a little while. I called and asked if George could come and pick up the dogs, because I felt it was going to rain. He said he was on his way. When he got to my cottage, he said, "Don't worry. I will keep them for the night, while you are at the hospital with your friend." Then he drove off with the dogs.

Driving to the hospital in the next town, I felt a great sadness come over me and said a prayer for strength. When I got there, Anita was settled into a room and had a bunch of tubes attached to her, and oxygen too.

I held her hand and she said, "Mary, I am scared to die. Please stay with me tonight?"

I said I would. "Would you like to pray with me?"

She said, "Yes." So we prayed together. She said, "You have been so wonderful since I came to your home and have taken good care of me, and I will miss you."

As tears ran down my cheeks, I said, "I will miss you, too. Would you like me to tell you something I have learned?"

She said, "Yes."

"When I had an operation to remove a fatty tumor, it was very strange, because I did not remember even being put under. Then, just as suddenly, I was awake. I asked Yahweh and he told me that it is like you had died, but the only difference is you wake up on the Other Side. Well, I don't know why I have been so afraid all of these years, and from then on, I was not. Anita, I am going to help you every step of the way, so you do not feel fear, all right?"

She said, "Thank you."

"Now, when you get to the Other Side, you will be as solid as you and I are right now. You can eat and drink and even sleep. There is a waiting place for souls to go when they leave this world and go to a much higher dimension. I know that you will love it there. Also, your loved ones will be waiting with open arms to greet you."

As you readers may know, I talked to my friend all night until morning.

When the first glow of the morning sun came into the hospital room, I felt it was her time. She grabbed my hand and then asked for a hug, and I gave it to her. She said, "Please tell Mr. Graves when you get home, and ask him to come and fetch me, okay?"

I said that I would, then she said, "Oh my goodness, I can see a beautiful rainbow of crystals in the distance. Is that what you were talking about?"

I said, "Yes, it was."

She said, "I do not have fear any more." She smiled at me and said goodbye, and that she would visit me soon and tell me everything. Then she was gone.

At that moment my tears did not come; I was at peace. My friend was at a place where she was awaiting her turn to cross over.

I rang for the nurse and the doctor just then, and they came into the room. While they were working to prepare her, I left and came home.

When I arrived home, I called the mortuary and told them about Anita and that the hospital would let them know when to pick up her remains. I asked Yahweh to please take good care of my friend, and then he spoke to me.

"My child, please listen to me now. We will be flying in my silver ship to her new home."

I said, "Thank you, and amen," and just sat there, for I was very weary, after being awake all night. I called George and said I was back and asked him to bring the dogs back.

He said, "Yes."

I told him I might take a nap for a little while because I had stayed awake all night. "So please put them in the fenced yard for me."

He said, "Yes, I will."

I didn't even go upstairs. I just got a blanket and went to the sofa to lie down. I went to sleep right away.

CHAPTER 3

*I*WOKE UP AND HEARD Max howling, so I brought the dogs in and hugged them both, to comfort them. I knew that it would take a while for Max to adjust to not having his mama around any more, but we both would have to work together on this. Max was a very sweet dog and had a loving temperament. Soon he would be all right. Animals have feelings, too, as well as souls, and we all need to respect them for these things.

Mr. Graves called to say he went and picked up the remains of Anita that afternoon and was preparing her now. She had asked to be cremated and her ashes strewn over the property where her new home was. He then said, "It will be a couple weeks before I can give you the ashes."

I said, "Thank you, and it's all right, for I have arrangement to make," and I hung up the phone.

I had not eaten since last night, so I fed the dogs and then had my supper and sat down to read my mail, then decided it could wait until tomorrow. The rest of the evening I just sat and read Anita's mail. To my joy, the bills were all taken care of before she moved to the cottage.

I put the mail aside because it was late, and then let the dogs out one more time. I covered the birds and by that time the dogs wanted back in, so I let them in. They followed me upstairs and now I had one dog on the right and one on the left side of my bed, on the rug, and we all went to sleep.

On Wednesday morning it was raining softly, but that was all right for me; I love the rain. As always, I let both of my dogs out in the morning, and when they wanted in, I let them in, dried them off, and they came up to me wagging their tails. Both had their mouths open like a panting smile.

I said, "All right, I know you are hungry, so here's your food." After they ate, they went and got cozy by the fire. I guess that Max was feeling better because he knew he was not abandoned. I realized something; I was lucky all of these years with Sparkle, because she was not spayed, and I'd had her for seven years. Then it dawned on me: Was Max fixed?

Something came to my mind then: "These dogs are to produce service dogs for people in need of them. But do not worry, this only has to be done for three years, because then there will be enough puppies to supply the demand. Then you can have them spayed and neutered."

I said "thank you" to this voice. "This is indeed an honor and I do believe that it's a gift from my beloved friend Anita."

As I went about my regular things I do in the morning, the sun came out and smiled its "good morning" to me. After breakfast I put a leash on both of my sweet dogs and got in the truck and drove to town.

My first stop was the vet's, to have my dogs checked out, and I asked Skip, "Is Sparkle all right to be a mother of service dogs?"

He said, "Yes, indeed, and we have a special need for them. Just the other day a letter was sent to me, asking me if he knew anyone who would provide service dogs."

Then I said, "Well, I am willing, because I read somewhere that the two breeds of dogs I have make a wonderful combination, due to their loving temperaments."

Skip said, "This is right. I have checked both of these dogs out, and they are very healthy."

I said, "I have a feeling that we just may have a bunch of puppies, but we just have to wait and see what happens in the next few weeks."

"Thank you, Skip, for your help, and for giving them their shots that they needed."

We then went to the mortuary to make arrangements for a memorial service for my friend in four weeks. I parked the truck and left a window open for air, and then I went to the library. I told Grace the news and she was so sad. Then I said that I knew that Anita was looking down on us all and she was very happy now and healthy. We made plans together and set a date for the chapel service.

Afterwards, I hugged Grace and left. Next I stopped at the beauty shop and confirmed my appointment for 11:00 in the morning, then left. After that, I went to the post office and canceled Anita's P.O. box. I checked my own mail and put it in a special cloth bag I had bought the other day.

For some reason I had to call George at the farm on my cell phone, to see if he was home. He said, "Come on over. We would love a visit with you. Did you bring your dogs with you?"

I said, "Yes."

He then said, "Good. I have something for them."

I told the dogs, "George has a gift for the two of you." I knew they understood. They both barked.

I went to the farm and parked the truck, then got my dogs out of the back, and we went to greet George and Georgia. They were extra happy, for some reason. They took one of the dogs each and placed a brand new collar on them with their names and a new leash to match. They gave them each a new toy that they could not destroy.

"Thank you both so much for doing this for me. You must really love my two babies a lot."

They said, "Yes, we do, because we had a lot of fun with them when they were here. On the day we took care of them, they were being more than just loving pals, so I think that in a few weeks you may notice that Sparkle is gaining weight."

I said, "Yes? I just today took them to the vet to have them checked out and asked him if service dogs were in great need. He said, 'Yes, very much.' And now that you have noticed this happened, it is confirmed. With both of their true breeds, these will make wonderful guide dogs."

"Yes, and we are glad that you have agreed to do this."

And I said, "I can only do this for a couple more times, because I don't want to overbreed them."

Then George said, "That's good, because they are older now and need to retire after this."

"You know, I can hardly wait to see the puppies. I know they will be so cute."

George and Georgia said the same thing.

"Well, I have to go now, and it looks like I will need a special place close to the house that will be a nice warm place when these little ones are born. Goodbye now. I will talk to you later, and again thank you both so much."

Well, this year was going to be a very fruitful year, yes, indeed. I felt like getting a lunch to go, so stopped by the diner. I ordered a Monte Cristo sandwich to go. Then, when I got my order, I went to the pet store for dog food because I needed a lot today, then drove home.

As soon as I got in the door, the phone rang and I hurried to answer it. It was Mom and Dad, and I told them what happened. They said they were so sorry.

Then I asked, "How can I help you, Dad?"

"Well, we want you to know that we will arrive on February 28, and so will your daughter and son. This is going to be a very busy weekend for all of us."

I then said, "You don't have to do this all alone, as far as moving things into your new home, because the townspeople will be there before you are, and put everything in place for all of you, and I will be there, too. We will even have something for you to eat because I know you will be very hungry. The town diner is providing this for all three of the families. I can hardly wait for you to get here. I guess the moving company is already on the way."

"It will arrive two days before we do."

I said, "Good. Everything will be in place when you get here, and then you can just relax, so please tell my son and daughter the same thing."

"Yes, we will, and goodbye, dear."

"Oh, I forgot, the Tuesday after you are here, which is March 1st, we will be having a memorial service for Anita, and then we will be throwing her ashes from the hill by the chapel. Would you like to attend?"

"Well, yes, dear, we would."

"We will all be together soon. I love you both so much." When I hung up the phone, I put my dogs outside and then ate my sandwich before it got cold. I got a dolly and transported the dog food to the pantry because they were big bags. Then I brought the other things inside and put the truck away. As I did this, I looked at Anita's car and said that I had better see to it soon. And also the cottage. It will be hard to face, but today I had other things to think about.

I wondered, "What makes this town so special? Soon I will have to look into this." There were a lot of puzzles and mysteries that I needed to solve. It was all part of the wonderful puzzle, for my awakening.

I needed to read my mail, so I took it into the other room and sat down after I made a new fire in the fireplace. It seemed as if my mind kept drifting for some reason, because I just could not concentrate on what I was reading. So I just sat back and closed my eyes to see why this was happening.

All of a sudden, a bright picture came into view, showing me what was troubling me. I could see several souls in front of me, saying to me, "You are the one to lead them and guide them in this town. You are to teach them the truth as to why they are here gathered all together. They were chosen and guided here, as well as you. These ones are all from your home in the skies. They want you to seek them out, because deep down they know why you are here. Does this help, my child?"

I said, "Yes, it really does."

"You already know, and you must bring this deep knowing into your everyday life. Names are not important at this time, but the awakening is. We must go now, and meditate on this, and you will find what you need to know to teach them. You will find that you will not need any help with this, because you will take one step at a time. We will talk again. Love, the souls."

My eyes suddenly opened to a bright understanding that was indeed a revelation of unending knowledge. I was truly blessed. I did not truly realize what all my duties were and still had a lot to do. But I was so happy to have the honor of doing this for mankind, and before I got up, another voice came to me: "You are the healer of minds and bodies and souls, and this is ongoing."

This was a lot to think about, but I was glad that I knew what was expected of me.

It was getting into late afternoon now and I began to start supper because I wanted to eat early tonight. Something simple would be just fine. I told the dogs, "I love you so much," and gave them each a big hug. We all sat in the living room and just enjoyed each other's company before going up to bed. Then I did the nightly duties and then we all went to sleep.

The sun was bright the next morning as I got out of bed, so I got dressed right away and went downstairs. This was my hair day, so I did some light housekeeping after breakfast and put my dogs outside to enjoy the sunshine while I was gone.

Soon it was time to leave and I made sure everything was turned off and then left for town, this time driving the golf cart that had been charging all night. It was fun to be in the golf cart again. I felt like I was in a convertible..

I was just in time for my hair to be done and walked inside. This time I had the full works done, mainly because of the tea party I was going to tomorrow afternoon. Nancy was there, too, and was having the same thing done to her hair. We talked until it was our turn and she said she would pick me up at 11:30 to go to the tea party.

Oh, it felt so nice to be pampered, and Pat was so much fun to talk to. She said that they would all be at the memorial service on March 1st, and this was wonderful to me. It was going to be a very nice send-off for my friend Anita.

Soon I was all done, and I paid for the great job Pat did for me, and left. I still had a hostess gift to buy, so I headed to the gift shop and picked out some cute tea spoons that had a little dragonfly and a butterfly on the handles. I had them wrapped for the hostess, then went to the diner and had a late lunch after going to the post office.

Then I had a thought: "It's time that I have my own mailbox set up in front of my cottage and have someone make it *look* like a little cottage. That, to me, would be very fitting." This I would check into on Monday. I had a nice salad that day and herb tea, and afterwards I drove my golf cart home.

Yes, it was a very nice day indeed.

When I came home from getting my hair done — the works, in order to look nice for tomorrow — I parked my golf cart in a special place in the barn and plugged it in. My dogs were glad to have me home and I gave them both a nice hug, and then brought them inside. It was getting time to fix supper but first I spent some time with Sparkle and Max. I was too excited to eat a big supper, so I just had soup, a salad and herb tea after feeding my dogs. For the rest of the evening I just sat in the living room and read my mail and relaxed before going to bed.

Early in the morning I did a good house-cleaning after taking care of all my pets. Then I went out to the mini cottage and decided to box up Anita's few belongings. After that, I labeled the boxes and placed them in a corner of the attic, for I did not want to part with them just yet.

I then called someone and asked what to do about my friend's car. They told me that next week they would come over and look at it and see what shape it was in. So I said thank you and after it got checked over I would donate her car to a young person for their first car. They said that was a great idea.

After this was all done, it was nearing time for Nancy to drop by and pick me up, so I went upstairs and took a bath, then got dressed. When I was ready, I looked in the mirror to see how I looked and was very surprised. This was going to be fun.

Soon Nancy knocked on my door and we left. My dogs were already outside, so I knew they would be all right. Nancy looked stunning in her new outfit and we were quite the ladies.

Soon we arrived at the party, and we all introduced ourselves to one another. We placed our gifts on a special table and found our places where the name cards were set. The hostess took pictures of all of us, so we could have keepsakes of the party.

The tea was served and the many little different heart-shaped cut-outs to make the sandwiches fit the theme of the party. Then we played a game to see how many herbs we could name, and they had a prize for the one with the most names. To my surprise, I won a tiny tea pot and tea cup charm on a bracelet. I just adored it. Next, the dessert was brought in on two-tier plates. They were so clever the way the hostess formed them for the party. There were heart-shaped cakes with light pink frosting and tiny flowers on them. She had little tarts with strawberries and a certain kind of filling and white truffles. This was all so very beautiful.

The hostess's name was Lola and she had blond hair and blue eyes. As the party drew to an end, Lola opened all her gifts, and I took pictures of this. Lola said, "I truly love these presents. They are lovely. I always wanted some of these." After the party, we all said our goodbyes and left.

This was indeed so much fun. Nancy drove me home and I thanked her for inviting me and then she drove off. It was late afternoon now when I got home and a Friday night, so I went upstairs and changed my clothes and put on my night clothes. Then I came down and let my dogs inside and fed them. I decided to have a tuna sandwich and carrot salad with iced tea. By this time I really felt the big day come on me, because I had done a lot before going to the party.

It was only nine at night, but I was tired. I let the dogs out for a bit and then brought them in and we all went upstairs and I got into bed. To my surprise, I was asleep the minute my head hit the pillow.

CHAPTER 4

O
N SATURDAY MORNING I slept in a little longer, until Sparkle and Max wanted out. Finally I said, "Okay, let them go."

I decided to first take care of my pets and then get dressed. Then I took a nap. Later on, I got up from my nap on the sofa and decided to go to town in my golf cart, to pick up my mail for the weekend. I would then ask what I should do to get a number for my country mail box that I wanted to place by the roadside. They gave me a form to fill out and I took it with me. Then I came right home because I felt like taking a walk.

When I got home, the dogs were really excited when they saw the leashes and I put them onto their collars. To my surprise, they didn't pull on the leashes, which made it better walking them. As we were walking we came to a meadow and there was a trail, so we followed to see where it led.

To my surprise, it was the same lake I had seen in my dream, and the same row boat was there. I said to myself, "Why not get in the boat and see where it takes us?"

We all got into the boat and I untied the line and then rowed the boat for a while. Then I did see a cave in the rocks of a mountain by the lake. I decided to row the boat inside, and it was the same cave with the rock formations inside.

I didn't get out of the boat this time and only observed the beauty. Then I knew where this was and would come another time alone as there was a light behind the rocks and I knew that what was behind there belonged to me from eons ago.

We then turned back and went back to the jetty, where all of us got out of the boat. My dogs waited while I tied the row boat to the jetty. We then returned to the cottage and I took the leashes off and put the dogs in the fenced yard.

After that, I put the golf cart in the barn and plugged it in. Then I went inside to make lunch. As I sat at the kitchen table I read my mail. I got a letter from Mandy, and she asked if she could stay at the little cottage when she came down to get married in June because she didn't want her husband-to-be to see her until the wedding on June 1st.

I thought I had better let her know right away, so I called her, and when she picked up the phone she was so excited to hear from me.

I said that I felt like I needed to let her know it would be wonderful to have her use the cottage. Then I asked, "Where will your parents stay when they come down for the wedding?"

She said, "I'm not sure."

I told her that we had a lovely bed-and-breakfast here in town for them, and if they liked I would ask Margie to hold some rooms for them. And also there was another one in town that her husband-to-be could use and his family could stay in. I could ask about that one, too. "It's in the country and has more rooms than the one close to town."

"Could you do this? That would be wonderful."

I said, "Sure. Tell them to call Shady Acres Bed-and-Breakfast and make reservations, and I will help by talking to them too. How many rooms do they need?"

She said, "About seven, for we are having a small wedding."

I said, "Mandy, would you like to have your reception here in my back yard, for the gardens will be in bloom then, and I can get everything ready for you. You just have to let me know what you want and the colors you want to use, and it's free."

She said, "Yes, yes, yes, I would love this."

"Okay then. Have your parents contact me, so we can make plans, all right? We have a lovely bakery here in town to make your wedding cake. Until then, please keep in touch, and oh yes, how many bridesmaids will you have?"

She said, "Three."

Then I said, "I have an attic with two bedrooms, and it is just perfect for them, for there are twin beds in each room."

"That would be wonderful."

"Well, goodbye now, and we will talk again soon." This, I said to myself, is going to be a lot of fun. The barn can be used for now as a place for the reception party, and is large, so they can dance, and I am so happy that George and his friends will be working on the barn because then part of it can be used for the reception and my cows can stay in the small pasture until after the party.

I needed a nap, so I took my nap on the sofa for a while. This was not very long. I soon got up because I needed to fix a dish for the Sunday pot luck. Then I cooked my supper and it was getting late, so we all went upstairs and went to bed.

Sunday service was wonderful and all my new friends were sad to hear of Anita passing so suddenly. I told them she was needed on the Other Side because she still had important work to do yet.

That afternoon at the potluck was so nice and I truly was getting to know all of my new friends in town. It was soon over for the day and I drove home. I had a relaxing day for what was left of it and took a nap.

I heard my guide talk to me, and she said, "Do you know what was in the cave when you made a visit yesterday in the row boat?"

I said, "Yes, I do know what is in there now."

She said, "This is good, but you must not say a word about this to anyone just yet."

I said that I understood.

"This is very good because, for now, your new friends have to wake up a lot more before this can be revealed to them."

"Thank you for telling me this."

"We will talk again soon."

It felt like rain because I had just heard some thunder and lightning outside. I checked the sky with a brightness of a searchlight. Soon I could hear the rain falling, so I went and let Sparkle and Max in because it surprised them, and even frightened them a little. In they came and they were shaking, so I made a fire in the fireplace and dried them off.

For some reason I had a craving for some popcorn and s'mores, and since the fireplace was going I could roast marshmallows. I fixed the popcorn and brought it into the living room and got cozy with a blanket over me, then watched the fire while eating my popcorn. When it was time for my s'mores, I roasted the marshmallows. I didn't turn on the television because of the thunder and lightning still crackling in the sky. I just wanted to enjoy the moment.

There was still some food left from the pot luck, so later I got a paper plate and ate my supper after feeding my dogs. It was getting late by now, and I thought it best to let Sparkle and Max out again. Then we all went up to bed.

Monday it was still raining, so I couldn't do much traveling. I called a man that makes cute things out of wood, and asked if he could make a mailbox that was big enough for a lot of mail, but looked like my cottage. His name was Bradley and he said, "Of course I can. How soon would you like it?"

I said, "Please don't rush because I have to make sure it's all right to do this."

He then said, "People around here have all kinds of different shaped boxes, and it's very legal."

I thanked him and then hung up the phone. Since it was raining, I called both of my friends to see if my friends' parents could book the whole inn for a wedding party on the weekend of June first. They said yes and told me to tell the ones involved to call and give the names of those that would be staying.

I called the bakery to see how much time they needed in advance to order a wedding cake, and she said, "Now is good." Then I called a florist to check. They said now was a good time as well. At least the parents would know who to call.

Then I had to call the restaurant and find out if they did catering for weddings, and they said yes, all they needed to do was let us know what type of foods they would want for the wedding. It was so good to get these things out of the way in advance, because last minute is bad news.

For some reason I felt I needed to call Jill, since she was getting married in May. As I punched the number for her phone someone knocked on my door. I stopped and hung up the phone. To my shock it was Jill. I said, "Oh my, I was just trying to call you because I felt I needed to ask you something. Come on in. What brings you out here? Aren't you going to open the book store?"

Jill said, "I closed my store for today, because I needed repairs done before Mandy comes in June."

She had something to ask me. "What is it, Jill? Can I be of help?"

Jill then asked me as we were sitting at the kitchen table, "Would it be all right if I have my wedding in your beautiful garden, because I have heard from the townspeople that it is so perfect."

I told her that was just what I was calling her about when she knocked on my door. "I wanted to know what type of wedding theme you had in mind, and also if you have made arrangements yet for your wedding cake and flowers, et cetera. And yes, you may have your wedding here and in the garden as this is what you would like."

She said, "Yes, I do, very much. My theme is country western. As far as the food, my parents thought it would be nice to just be casual and have a potluck. I have ordered my cake for May as well as the flowers. I made my own wedding gown in the western design. The men will have western type suits as well as the bridesmaids having western style gowns."

I said, "How nice that sounds. So I have a feeling that you will have a barbecue outside the barn."

She said, "Yes."

"Now I know the other reason that George and his friends and the people from town will be doing repairs of my barn. They knew about this, and you know what I think? It's a great idea. Who is going to do the ceremony?"

She then told me, "Grace."

"She will be doing the ceremony. Would you like to have some lunch while we're here making plans? It's noon now and I am hungry from all of this planning."

She said, "Yes, I would." We both worked together to make lunch, and then we sat down and ate together.

"It's too bad it's raining, I could take you out to see the barn and you could give me an idea how you want things arranged out there for the reception, but we can do that another time."

After a while, the two of us said our goodbyes and I said to myself, "I am almost like a wedding planner." My dogs were wanting out, even though it was still raining, so I let them out for a little bit, and then they wanted back in. It was still a little chilly, so I put another log on the fire. "Oh my," I said to myself, "I sure am going to be busy the next three months, and I can say one thing for sure: I am never bored. I guess I better call Mandy and give her the phone number of both inns and the bakery and flower shop and the caterer, because her parents will need this to start getting things planned for June."

Then I asked her, "What is your theme for your wedding?"

Mandy said, "Oh it is a Southern belle type wedding, and I will be going to the church in a carriage, holding an umbrella."

"Thank you. I was just going to ask how and what you would be driving to the church in on that weekend. I was thinking of the golf cart, but now that you have told me, Mandy, that's much better. Would you like me to ask if they have a carriage in town at one of the riding stables?"

She said, "Could you, please? That would be a great help. Dad will pay for that, since he will be giving me away."

"Then it's settled. I will contact them and have your dad call me in a week or so, to see about this, all right?" Then we finished our call and I sat down on the sofa, drew the blanket over me, and took a nap.

With this I had another dream, and Stands With Clouds was in my dream. He said, "There is a Native American village about three miles from town, and they would like for you to come and visit them. They want to give you a blessing, and restore your gifts as a medicine woman, because even though you are only a fourth Cherokee, you were a full Cherokee in a past life eons ago. This is why you had the single golden eagle visit your back yard when you lived in California. It was to wake you up to your heritage, and also, you have healing ability."

This was very dynamic for me; I was compelled to grow herbs. Then I woke up suddenly.

Next, I put on a jacket and boots and walked outside to the back garden to find a nice place to plant herbs in March. I found a perfect spot to form a medicine wheel-shaped herb garden and wondered if the climate was right for a lemon tree. That would be something to ask about later at the town nursery. Then I went back inside and started supper, and then fed my dogs and then called it a night, because even though I hadn't done any physical work today, I had used my brain a lot and it made me tired.

The last week had gone very fast and my parents would be arriving soon, as well as my son and my daughter. I wanted to be at their new farm to greet them.Hank at the hardware store called one morning and said that the moving van came and had asked where the farm was, and they were there now.

"Would you like to go there and let them know what goes where?"

I said, "Yes." Then off I went in my truck, and they had just pulled up when I arrived, so I directed them as to what went where. The townspeople came driving in too. They unpacked and put things away for my parents and even made up the beds. Then they left to go to my son's and daughter's farms, and I followed behind them, and the moving vans were just arriving in each place, so I went to each one, because they were a mile apart, and did the same.

When it was all done, I was pooped. I knew that my parents and son and daughter would arrive on Monday of March 3rd, so I had the weekend to rest up. Then I had an idea. As I was driving home I had the idea to have a barbecue in the barn on Sunday, to thank everyone for their help.

I then made plans to do that part of the potluck for after church. We would have hamburgers, hot dogs, and corn on the cob if I could find fresh corn this early in the season. So I called the general store to see if any had come in and they said no, so I decided on baked potatoes instead and I ordered them. I told Larry I would pick up what I needed for the Sunday pot luck today.

He said, "You don't have to do that. We will deliver this to you."

I said, "Thank you so much," and then hung up the phone.

After they delivered all my supplies on Saturday, I got busy baking homemade rolls for the hotdogs and hamburgers. I also had one of those barbecue pits brought out, for the large amount of people that would be coming on Sunday, as well as tables and chairs at the rental place in the next town. Now I was all set up.

It was getting late when all the baking was done. My dogs and I went upstairs and went to sleep.

The next morning I did what was normal each morning and then got dressed and went to church. After church I came home sooner than the rest, to get the charcoal started. To my surprise, the men from church were already there, doing that for me, and it was a good thing I had baked the potatoes the night before, because all I had to do was wrap them in foil and place them on the grill to get hot again.

The table and chairs were all set up and there were some tubs with ice for the soft drinks. Then everyone arrived, and we joined hands in a circle and said a blessing. We all dug in and got our food. This was so much fun.

I said to all of them before they left that I was so very grateful for all of their help with unpacking of my parents', and son's and daughter's belongings. They all said we were most welcome.

After they left and all was put away, I took a nap, for this was my very first of many parties to come. I enjoyed it all very much. There was some food left over from the potluck, so I got a paper plate and ate supper, and there was even meat left over. I gave my dogs the hamburgers and after we were done, we went up to bed.

It was March 1st, and the memorial service was going to be on Tuesday at the chapel and then the spreading of my friend's ashes. I had to get over to the horse farm to greet Mom and Dad, and then we were all going over to my son's and also daughter's places to greet them. I got dressed and fed my dogs and had my breakfast and drove a mile further from my place to my parents' place.

I waited until they drove into the yard. I was so excited that I just ran and hugged them as soon as they got out of their car. And Bruce, their collie, was there too. We all went into the farmhouse and we all looked into every room and were so glad to be together, to be close again like we used to be. After this, and putting Bruce in the fenced yard, we all drove to my son's farm and did a survey of their farmhouse, and then a mile to my daughter's farm.

After all of this, I drove my son back to his place as well as his wife, then Mom and Dad to their place. They all said they were very tired from the trip and were going to take a long nap, so I drove home and before I left, I told them what time the service was for the memorial of Anita, then went home.

The next day, I got up early and was not very hungry, so I put my dogs outside after I fed them. I only had coffee and toast. I got dressed and put the urn of ashes in my truck and drove to the church. Some flowers were delivered to the chapel and it was very beautiful in there. I sat with all of my family, and the service began.

Grace did a wonderful blessing of the ashes, and got up and said what a nice friend Anita was to me from all of those years. We all sang *Amazing Grace* and then filed outside to the higher part of the chapel grounds, where I opened the urn and let the ashes fly over the valley. I knew she was flying too, in another sense. This was quite an amazing experience.

We all went to the hall where all the food was gathered, and talked and ate our food that we all had brought, and then we enjoyed the rest of the service. After all this, we went home.

As I was driving home, all of this activity hit me all at once, and a voice said to me, "You better take it easy for a few days," and I said, "You are very right."

After arriving home, I put my truck away and went into the cottage and let the dogs inside. After that, I went upstairs and took a nap too. In the meantime, the parents and son and daughter were laying down for a nap, because it was like a whirlwind for the past couple of months, and if they didn't slow down, this was going to make them sick.

For the rest of the week little happened. We just took it easy. The new mailbox was delivered and I had them put it up, then paid them for a terrific job. After they left, I rested some more and decided to stay home until Sunday.

After church service on Sunday, I didn't go to the pot luck because it was my parents', son's, and daughter's first weekend in town. They invited me to their place for a family get-together.

When I got there after church, we were all gathered in my parents' big country kitchen. This was so nice for the first Sunday that we were together as a family. My dad asked me how I was coping with the loss of my friend.

I said, "Pretty well, due to all that has happened. It was so fast. I thought that Anita had more time. No wonder she was in a hurry to come to my place. I think she knew that the doctors mis-counted how long she had."

My mother said, "That sounds about right, because who knows better how you feel than you do about your own body?"

I said, "That's true."

Then my son said, "Well, Mom, she knew that her best friend would be there for her, and I know that she was very grateful for all of your loving help."

My daughter said, "Here, here!" in agreement.

We all started talking about how much we liked our new homes and farms. Then the topic went to the upcoming births of the new babies. My son-in-law said, "I am so happy to have a safe place to raise our children, where there is no threat of negative things happening to our babies. Our children need to be children. They don't need to be rushed into adulthood sooner than they are ready."

We all agreed with this. My daughter-in-law said that she, too, liked country life because the air was so clean and the water so pure. "The next season we will start planting a crop of corn and wheat and, maybe if we have room, alfalfa. But we will first start with corn, because for the present I have to cope with morning sickness."

I told her to try eating lightly in the morning and then gradually work up to something heavier to eat. "Get some ginger ale and soda crackers, but above all drink lots of water."

She said that was a very good idea.

Then I said, "After getting used to being away from the big city, I think your body will feel better, because of the smog and all of the preservatives in the food they have in the stores."

Both my daughter-in-law and my daughter agreed with this. My daughter said, "I am so glad I don't have morning sickness, because

I don't think I could handle that. When I was young, I was so sick, and I am glad to not be sick now."

After lunch all the men got up and looked around the stables, to decide just what to do when the horses arrived in a week or so. You see, when my father was young, he lived on a ranch with his parents. They knew how to handle them, so his dream was to have a different kind of stables, where there was not just horseback riding, but also old-fashioned sleigh rides for everyone in the winter, when the snow was on the ground, and carriage rides in the countryside in the spring and summer. They just wanted to go back to the old ways that were slower and more enjoyable for everyone. My son and son-in-law liked this idea as well.

We women were still in the kitchen discussing the up and coming birth of the babies. I was becoming a grandma for the first time. My mom would become a great-grandma. This was going to be a great celebration when all of these babies were born. My mom and I got into the subject of sewing, and we decided to work together and make baby quilts, as well as quilts for the up and coming winter months for our own beds.

Soon it was getting to be evening, and I said that I had to get home and let my dogs inside because my dog also would be giving birth to her puppies. I wanted to make sure she was well taken care of. I gave everyone a hug. The men of the family came in the back door at just the right time.

Then I was on my way. My son and his wife left shortly after this, as well as my daughter and son-in-law. They all had a big day and wanted to leave early. Each of them took some goodies home to eat just before going to bed that night.

CHAPTER 5

ONDAY MORNING I TOOK care of my dogs and birds, then put the dogs out and decided to have breakfast at the diner before doing my errands. This time I had Belgian waffles and sausage on the side, and it really tasted good.

Cindy had her break and sat down with me to have her coffee. She said, "May I come over next Saturday, for I am in much need of a walk in the country, and someone to talk to about my spiritual way of life. I don't have anyone to talk to about the happenings I have experienced. I feel that you will understand somehow."

I said, "Of course you can. And I, too, have things along the same line to talk about. In fact, why not come over Friday night, and stay overnight? It will be fun for us both."

Cindy said, "Thank you. I would enjoy that."

After I left the diner, I walked to the post office to put in a change of address for my new mailbox. So now, the following Monday, I would get my mail at home. The number was Rural Route 311, Highway 97, in between Al Goma and Klamath Falls. The town was a side road in between there. This was not shown on any map, since the town was small.

The next stop was the vet's. Skip asked how Sparkle was doing. I said, "She is doing just great." He told me to let him know the minute she was giving birth to the puppies, and bring her in, if possible. I told him yes, I would.

I then went to the pet store for supplies, and then to the general store to buy some things I was out of. They asked how my parents were doing, and I told them they loved it in their new place. Then I took my things and left.

I decided to go to the Native American village just down the road because of the dream I'd had. There was a small sign that was almost hard to see, and I turned left onto a dirt road and down a few miles to the village.

On arriving there, I parked my truck and went up to the first hut that was like a large gathering place, and asked to talk to Chief Dancing Sun.

When I said this, all of a sudden the entire group turned to me and one of them said, "We have been waiting for you to come. We know that you had a dream the other day because it was telepathic. We are glad you took the call and were open to these things. Please come and sit. We have much to tell you. You are called to reopen your gifts as a medicine woman. Do you remember the visits of the many golden eagles?"

I said I did.

"It is time to be awake to these medicine woman gifts. You are planning to make an herb garden in the shape of a medicine wheel. We know of this. We see you planning; soon we will come and help with the many different herbs to plant. We now wish to have a ceremony for you to give you your new Medicine Woman name."

Then they started singing in their Native Cherokee language and chanted with the drumming and dancing. They placed a special shawl around my shoulders, and then they placed a large quartz crystal, fan-type object, with a golden eagle feather attached to the crystal, into my hands.

One of them was burning sage and blessing me. Soon all the dancing and chanting and singing halted and they told me, "Your new name is Spirit Caller."

When this was over, they said, "In a few weeks, we will come and bring a horse that is white with many spots on her rump, called Many Stars. Now go and we will be by to show you soon how to make gardens."

After this honor I was numb and could hardly drive home, but I knew that my guides were helping me to cope with this new honor. I did get home safely, and after taking my last mail from my post office box and the other things from the store, I put the truck away, then let the dogs inside before I did anything else.

Then I sat down and ate a sandwich I'd gotten from the deli. Afterwards, I just pulled the blanket over myself and took a nap. I just wanted to let everything sink in. Then I fell asleep.

It was dark when I woke up. I must have really made a long trip some place when I slept. I said, "Oh my, I forgot about feeding my dogs." So I fed them and let them out afterwards and they came back in shortly. I decided to go up and get in bed to sleep the rest of the night, even though it was still early evening, and sleep I did.

I woke up at 6:00 in the morning very refreshed and also very hungry. Now you may wonder why I eat so much. If I do not eat, it makes me sick, so the reason I sleep a lot is because I am not very well in my older years. So I need this.

The day went as always, with the same order of duties, because it was Friday. After taking care of what I did every morning, I got the golf cart out and went to town. I needed some supplies for the walk Cindy and I would be taking on Saturday morning, and didn't have a backpack and water container. Then, after leaving the hardware store, I went to the diner and asked if Cindy owned a backpack. She said she did, so I told her to please bring it with her tonight.

The next stop was the general store for items of food for the hike we were going on Saturday morning. I got some things for the supper for the two of us. By then it was Friday afternoon and I headed home. After getting home, I put everything away, and then put the golf cart away and plugged it in. Next, I went in the back door of my cottage this time, and the dogs came in when I did. We went into the living room after I gave them each a treat and we rested.

I knew it would be Monday before I would start to get my first mail in my mailbox on the road. I knew a lot of it would be from Saturday and there would be a lot of mail. For some reason it came to mind to pack my backpack now and have it done with, and I remembered to have a first aid kit and blanket, a flashlight and my canteen, and a lightweight emergency shortwave radio to call on. It would also be a good idea to let someone know my location, just in case.

I called my parents to let them know about where we would be, and if I didn't call on our return, to please take care of the dogs. When this was done, I felt better. I took a late lunch and sat down to rest. I then drifted off to sleep.

I must have been really tired, for the knocking on my front door jolted me awake. I got up and answered the door to find Cindy standing there. I said, "Come on in," and then told Cindy I had been sleeping. "It was a longer nap than I intended. We will have to fix supper together."

She said, "That's okay. That would be fun."

As we were fixing supper I asked, "Does anyone know, just in case we get stranded, where you were going?"

She said, "Yes."

I said, "Good, for I did the same thing. We can never be too careful."

After eating, we got into our night clothes and went downstairs and had a nice time talking in front of the fire. She then asked me about some things she had seen in the past few years, for it was hard for her to keep to herself any longer. She said, "For the past few years when I take my walks in the country, something would make me look up to the sky, and not far above me were several shining silver disks moving about. It was so fun to watch them. I was not afraid at all, and with this a pleasant voice would speak to me." Then she asked, "Have you ever had this happen to you?"

"Yes, I have," I said, "when I was very young, and I did not tell my parents about it. You know, it's finally nice to be able to share this because I know it's for a reason, and I am supposed to do something. Lately, since I have moved here, I have had interesting things happen when I take my walks, and I have encounter dreams as well. And then when I am awake, when I am alone, a voice would speak to me. In fact, there are three different ones and they tell me they are my guides."

"Oh, my, I have been getting this too."

As we were talking, I heard a voice and got a message for us. While we were talking, one of my guides came through and wanted me to tell you all of this:

"My dear enlightened ones, you have been brought together at this time because you are of like spirits. You are both from the stars many light-years away from Earth. You are both in training now, and as soon as you are even more awake, we will tell you where this is, and your star names. You are both star seeds. You were born to Earth parents to do big works for mankind, to awaken the other star seeds. This is all for now, so the both of you need to keep doing what you are doing and will be given instructions as you sleep or meditate in your alone time. Blessings to both."

"Wow," we said. Finally after all of these years, we had an answer to why these things are happening.

We were both sleepy, so we went up to bed after letting the dogs out again, then bringing them back in. We both said our prayers before going to sleep and got in bed and fell asleep right away.

In the morning the sun was up and it was nice and warm. We both got dressed after refreshing ourselves and doing what we did in the morning. Then we came downstairs. Cindy let the dogs out while I was making coffee and starting breakfast. The dogs wanted in, so Cindy let them in, then fed them. After they came in, I put extra water outside for them.

Before we were ready to leave, we both sat down for a nice big breakfast and said the blessing. Then after this, we made sure we both had a lot of snacks and water in our canteens. We each also had on a jacket, a hat, boots and gloves, for you never know. We helped each other put on our backpacks, and then put the dogs outside.

Finally, we were on our way for the day's adventure. As we walked down the country road, we came to the dirt path that I told Cindy about. Now that I had a better look at my surroundings, I noticed that this area was the meadow in my dream, and there was a stream running from the mountains in the distance toward the stream that runs through my property. It was about a mile to the calm lake where the jetty was, and the same rowboat.

When we got there, we both got into the boat and took turns rowing it after untying the rope from the jetty. As we rowed into the cave I had told Cindy about, she said, "This is so beautiful. It's like many jewels shining as bright as day."

Then we saw a jetty inside the cave. Cindy got out first and tied the boat to the jetty and then I got out. We both saw a path and followed it.

Then a voice said to the both of us: "You have both earned the gift of knowledge and wisdom. We will allow you both to see what is behind the formations today, but remember this, you must never divulge what you find to anyone, because this belongs to Mary from eons ago, and also there is another craft that is hidden that is for someone you are yet to meet, and her name is Sara, but this you will all know later on." The voice also said that this would stay only between them and no others.

All of a sudden the formation in front of us opened up, and what we saw was a golden spacecraft, enough for two people, and the dome of the craft was light blue. We were both so honored to see this. It brought tears to our eyes and it was a deeply humbling and breathtaking sight.

Then the door opened in the craft and we both walked inside to look around. It was for our eyes only. The voice said to us again, "You still have more lessons to learn, Mary, to remember how to fly this craft, and Cindy, you as the navigator, you still have lessons to learn yet. But before you go, there is an opening at the right of this secret cave that has two objects inside that you must wear at all times."

We both got out of the craft, and the door closed. We both saw the opening and saw the two pendants of pure gold with a triangle and three suns on it. So we put them on, then took one last look at the spacecraft and went out the door. As we did, a voice said again, "This time after you leave this cave, there will be a rock-like door that will close the opening."

We both walked to the boat that was at the jetty in the cave. I got in and then Cindy got in and removed the line. And then we rowed out of the opening of the cave. Then the voice said to us, "Use the pendant by touching the gemstone in the middle at the same time, and the sliding door of rock will close."

So we did this after we left the cave opening. After touching the gemstone in the middle of the pendant and watching the rock door close, we were on our way back. We were both so overwhelmed, we were without speech.

When we got to the jetty, where we began our ride, we got out and tied up the boat. Then we realized something: We needed to find a place to hide the boat, and then we saw a tiny opening in some rocks and moved the row boat to this place. And this, too, had a sliding rock door, and so we did the same thing.

As we were walking toward the path we saw a nice shaded area with a small waterfall trickling down the side of the rocks, where we sat down and ate our lunch. We were so shocked at the wonder of it all that we just ate our lunch in silence. When we were done, we walked back to the cottage.

Soon we were there and Cindy said, "I shall never forget this wonderful day and I know that we need to talk as often as we can, so we can share what we are learning." Then Cindy went into the cottage and gathered up the things she had brought with her. We hugged and said our goodbyes, and Cindy drove off.

I went inside the cottage afterwards, then let the dogs in, took off the backpack and removed the things from inside to clean them. Then I repacked the backpack for another time and put it away. Next, I took off the boots and jacket and put them away.

Before sitting down to relax, I called my parents. I had to let them know I was home. After resting for a while, I read my large bunch of mail and then fixed a bunch of things for the potluck at church tomorrow. I ate my supper and did the things I always did, and then let the dogs back in and we all went to bed.

Sunday went by with the chapel service and wonderful message from Grace, and also the potluck. Soon the day was over and another day had started. Unknown to me, my parents were planning a surprise birthday party. I would be the age of 68 on the 17th of March, and there was already a celebration in town that would happen on my birthday. So this would top the frosting on the cake for me. There would be dancing from the dance company with Irish dancing, and other things. My parents knew how much I liked this sort of thing. We were all Irish.

On Monday morning George called and said that he and his crew were coming over to work on the barn, and he also said they would be working most of the week, building a chicken coop and a fenced-in place for the goats. They would also build a couple rooms in the hay loft to be guest rooms, because the men needed a place to sleep the night before the wedding in June.

This was good. There was going to be four bridesmaids that would use the attic room, and attendants for the groom needed a place to stay, so the loft was perfect. Mandy had called me Sunday night and told me this, so I was glad to know about it in advance.

I was able to find four second-hand twin beds for the men. There was a bathroom added to the loft of the barn too. I knew this was going to cost a lot, but thank goodness my parents came and helped me with expenses, since I was doing this to help so many people, and they were proud of me for being selfless like this.

I found out it would take two weeks instead of one week to get all of these things built, but since there were over one hundred or so people doing this, because of their many talents, the work went a lot faster.

Soon it was my birthday and I wondered what I should do for myself today. Cindy called just at that thought and invited me to lunch, so it was good that I was dressed in my special green outfit for the celebration in town.

Cindy knocked on my door, then we both left, and it was good that I had just put my dogs out. As we drove I noticed that Cindy was unusually silent, but I didn't pry because I knew that Cindy must have had something on her mind.

When we got to town, we parked at the town square and got out. Then we walked to the large Gazebo in the center, where I saw my parents and waved at them. All of a sudden as we walked into the gazebo, almost the whole town said, "Happy Birthday!" to me and sang to me. I was truly surprised at all of this, and I cried tears of happiness.

The party began with all kinds of Irish music, and there was a cake and many gifts from everyone who knew me over the past few months. Soon the celebrations started with Irish dancing, with a parade and all kinds of fun things to do, and since it was a holiday they had Irish ale. Knowing some would probably have too much, they had carriage rides home for the ones who drank too much ale. Soon it was all over and Cindy helped me put all my gifts in my car.

The day after my birthday, I needed to get out after breakfast and take a walk. The main reason was that I had eaten a lot at my party and needed the exercise. This time I took my dogs with me because they needed it too.

I put a leash on each dog and we were on our way. As we walked, I said to my, dogs, "I am so sorry I have not taken you for a walk very much, dear ones, but life has been busy. This time, instead of going the way we used to walk, we're going across the highway in front of the cottage. How does this sound?"

Then my dogs' tails wagged happily. I saw a road leading down a dirt road near a forest that was on the left side of the road. This was truly a beautiful spot, and the fragrance was fantastic coming from the fir trees. It was early spring and so much new life was all around with the dogwoods in bloom.

Soon we came to a fork in the road, and in between the forked road was an old cottage, almost the same as mine, only this one had double doors, like the Bed-and-Breakfast had. Sadly, this cottage had not been in use for a long time and the growth in the garden was in need of loving care.

I said to the dogs, "Let's take a look and see what this lovely place is like." I crossed over the curved bridge and then another one, and I could see that no one lived there any more. I tried the door knob to see if it was locked, and to my joy it was not locked, so I opened it and walked in.

There was dust and cobwebs everywhere, so I grabbed a broom nearby and got rid of some of the webs, then told my dogs to sit while I explored this cottage on the inside.

Then a voice said to me, "I am so glad you are here, because my place I loved so much is in need of help and a new owner. But the one I have in mind lives in a town in California. Her name is Sara. There is one lady that knows her, and this is Grace from your town chapel. Please contact her and give her this message, because she knows where Sara lives."

I said that I would do this and also have someone come and clean the inside of the cottage, and some gardeners to bring the outside garden back to the way it used to be.

Then the voice answered, "This would be wonderful, for, you see, I am giving my cottage to Sara as a gift for all her hard work of taking care of her mother. She does not know that I am aware of this, but since I am on the Other Side, I know these things. When you talk to Grace, and she makes contact with Sara, please ask her to ask Sara to help me get crossed over."

I said I would do this. The woman continued to talk. "Sara is the one who will teach and lead all of you. She is the one the town has been waiting for all of these years, and thank you for coming today. You are very special too, and you and Cindy will be taking classes with Sara, and working with her side by side. This is after Sara moves to the town of Welcome Home. I must pull back now, and I know you need to continue your walk with Sparkle, because when you get home Sparkle will be giving birth to her puppies today."

I said farewell because I knew I needed to get Sparkle home soon.

When I returned to the cottage, I called the vet and told him that Sparkle was acting strangely. "And I have a feeling she will be giving birth. Should I bring her in now or wait?"

Skip said, "Bring her now, so we can keep an eye on her."

So right away I got out my truck and gently helped Sparkle inside, and then put Max in the back yard. I told him, "Don't worry, I will be back in a little bit."

Then off I drove to the animal hospital. When I arrived, Skip came out with his helper and they carried Sparkle inside, and Skip said, "There is no reason for you to stay. We will call you on your cell phone and let you know what happens."

I thanked him and went home. When I got home, I called Grace to tell her what I had found out today. Then Grace said "Yes, I do know her, and will contact her this evening and give her the news. Thank you for telling me this, and I will call you tomorrow on Saturday, and will tell you what happened when Sara gets this news. So bye now, and thank you so much for this message."

After the call I could not relax because of Sparkle. Then I said to myself, "I should pray, so that I know that Yahweh can help me." After this I felt much more relaxed.

Then it was getting toward night and I knew that I should eat, but first I fed Max, then just made a grilled cheese and had tomato soup. After this, I let Max out and shortly after that brought him back in. I decided to go up to bed and Max followed.

I slept a fitful night, but at about 6:00 the next morning I got a call from Skip that the birth went well, but he had to take the puppies by C-Section, and also had to remove the uterus of Sparkle because she was up too much in age and may not last through another bunch of puppies.

I said, "Can I come and see her and the puppies this morning?"

Skip said, "Yes, but please wait until noon, because she and the puppies are resting now."

I said, "Yes, of course I will." After I hung up the phone, I felt very sad for Sparkle, so I knew it was for the best. I fixed my breakfast and fed Max. I said to him, "You are a proud papa of seven puppies. How great is that?"

He barked once and lay close by her to rest, because he, too, was worried about Sparkle and missed her a lot.

The phone rang and I answered it. It was Grace. "I have had a wonderful talk with Sara last night and she said to me that she is very tired of living in the town she is living in, and she would like to have a happy chance to live in a better place. She will be making arrangements to move as soon as she can. Her mother needs a nice place to spend her last years on earth, and this would be perfect for her as well. Her mom's house is being invaded by termites, and if this keeps up, the house won't be livable much longer. I gave Sara your phone number so she can call you and ask about the cottage. I hope this was all right."

I said, "Of course it is. Well, I am a grandma to seven puppies. They were born in the animal hospital this morning. She had to have a C-section, for she was weak. After the puppies were born, she had to have her uterus removed, so there won't be any more puppies, but at least these will bring some people comfort when they are old enough to be trained."

Grace said, "This is wonderful that you are doing this, and I will pray for Sparkle and her puppies, that they all get well soon. Goodbye."

I hung up the phone, then let Max outside to exercise. It was about noon now, so I got out my truck to go visit Sparkle and the new puppies. When I arrived at the animal hospital, I parked my truck and went right in. Skip came up to me, and led the way to see Sparkle. When I saw them, I said, "How cute! I know that after they are old enough to train, the puppies will learn very fast. If I could afford them, I would keep them, but I already have more than enough with the cows and chickens and goats to take care of. I was wondering, Skip, if Max would make a good dog to breed with other female dogs like Sparkle?"

He said, "Yes."

Then I said, "Let me know, because when more pups are needed for training, this is what my friend Anita would have wanted for me to do. But right now Max is still mourning his mistress, but when he's feeling better I will donate Max for a very good cause. How long will it be until I can bring Sparkle home with her puppies?"

Skip said, Tuesday next week."

I said, "Thanks for doing this for me. How old do they have to be, to begin training?"

Skip said, "Six months. I forgot to mention there was an eighth puppy, and it was very small. She is being kept in the place for newborn pups."

I said, "That is the one I will keep for me, if that's all right."

He said, "Yes, that would be fine, because she is very small. We are letting her suckle her mama, so she has the mother's milk, so I guess that's it for now. I guess I better go. See you and Tuesday."

I said, "I better go have some lunch. All this excitement has made me hungry." I then drove to the diner and had a hamburger and fries and a coke.

Cindy was there and talked to me. We filled each other in on what happened since the weekend. After eating, I left and went to the nursery to ask about who could come out to the cottage across from me down the dirt road, and get the front and back gardens ready for Sara to move in and what they would charge for this. They said, "We have a special policy for newcomers to town, and it's free."

Then I asked, "Is it too late in the season to dig up roses to transport to a new town?"

They said, "Tell the new owner to just be careful as she digs them up, and make sure she puts them in water a few days before she moves. Then have her place damp newspapers around them for traveling with a plastic bag around them and some newspaper, and they should be just fine."

I said, "Thank you very much, and I think she will be moving in about three weeks from now, depending on how her business goes. Bye now."

Then I went to a place where you can hire cleaning ladies, in the next town, and it was the same — for new people it is *free*. "Wow!" I said to myself, "I sure got a lot taken care of today. Now I need to find a new mail box for me to put on the road. Then everything will be nearly set."

The next stop was the General Store for food supplies. I was out of a lot of things. I got out at my Mom and Dad's home, then went home and brought Max in the house. After putting everything away, I called Grace and said I would not be at church on Sunday because I had a very busy week and needed to rest

I lay down on the sofa with Max on the floor and we both took a long nap. As I was about to fall sleep, a voice spoke to me: "Child, you must rest more than you have lately, because if you don't, you are going to end up in the hospital. You need to eat more than three meals a day, for you have not done this. You need to eat six meals a day. Don't feel bad about letting someone help you, all right? I must go now, and had to warn you."

I then said, "Thank you." I was feeling a little under the weather. Then I was fast asleep.

Later, after a good rest, I woke up and started my supper, then fed Max. For some reason, after doing all of this, I felt that something was wrong, but I wasn't sure what it was. Then I said, "Whatever it is, I will know by morning."

When I ate my supper and cleaned up the kitchen, I said to Max, "Let's watch some television for a while." After that I looked for something good to watch, gave up, and let Max out and then in again before going upstairs to bed, and then we both went up to bed.

This time on Sunday morning, I slept much later than I had for a long time, but that was all right. I needed the rest. I woke up at 9:00 in the morning. It came to me what was bothering me. Deep down, it was my health, so now I knew when I heard the voice yesterday, it was true what I felt. Thank goodness I was given a warning. Then I said, "I'd better make an appointment with the doctor on Monday. I'm going to make this my lazy day and sit around all day in my night clothes."

I knew somehow I would need to do something. It was not my nature to be lazy. I went downstairs to let Max out. I uncovered my birds and fed them, then let Max in and fed him, and had a nice breakfast. I saw a bird that was not from this area. It was a Baltimore oriole. Then I saw some bluebirds flying around and having a wonderful spring morning. I loved all birds, but this one was fun because they made nests in whatever they could find, like a hat hanging on a porch, or anything of that nature, and when they had their young ones, it was cute to have a close view of them on the porch feeding their young. Yes, nature is so much fun to watch, when we take time to notice what they do.

Soon I got another cup of coffee and for me this was odd because I am a one-cup person. I took it into the sunroom and looked out the window and just relaxed. Just then the phone rang and I answered it because I brought it in the sunroom with me.

To my surprise, it was Sara, who said, "I hope I am not too early with my call."

I said, "No, it is all right. I have been up for a while and am being a little lazy this morning. Grace told me you would be calling me last night or today. It's good to hear from you for the first time."

Sara then said, "I'm calling to ask what you saw when you looked at the cottage."

I then told her what I had seen a day or so ago when out walking. Then I said, "You sound like you know something I am not aware of. Please tell me what you know."

Sara then told me the dream, and after she was done she said, "It was like I told you just now."

I said, "Yes, but I have not had a chance to see where the boat is, for I was not there very long." Then I asked Sara, "Before you move here, would you like to visit me next weekend, so you can see for yourself?"

Then Sara said, "Yes. I would love this. I will be there on Friday, if it's all right with you. I will have a friend look after my mother and my dog a few days, so I can get away. I have to take either a bus or a small plane to your area. Is there a small airport close by?"

I said, "Yes."

Sara said, "Then that's what I will do. I will fly up there because it does not take as long."

Plans were made, and I would pick her up at the small airport three miles out of town on Friday afternoon. Then we said our goodbyes and hung up the phone. I then sat down to enjoy the rest of my day.

CHAPTER 6

MONDAY CAME AND WENT as always, and then on Tuesday, after everything was done, I went to the animal hospital to pick up Sparkle and her seven pups and take them home. When I got there and went inside, Skip had a large smile on his face.

I said, "You sure look happy this morning. What has happened to make you this way?"

He said, "I just got some wonderful news. I got a call today from the people who train puppies, and they are thrilled to have these puppies when they are six months old. Also, they are sending a young female golden retriever over to continue breeding more pups, so this plan is going to be a good thing for the blind and disabled folks in wheelchairs, and we all thank you so much for your help in this. Also, the youngest pup that was a runt will be going home with you today, as well as the others, and I am going to go and bring Sparkle in now, because she has missed you. Be right back."

Soon in came Sparkle, and I bent down to give her a nice hug, and Sparkle licked my cheek. She had a very happy look on her face and knew she was going home. I asked what instructions there were for taking care of all of them, and Skip gave them to me.

With the help of Skip and some others, we took Sparkle and the puppies out to the truck, but before leaving, I asked, "When will they be sending the young female dog?"

He said, "In six months."

I said, "Good. Max will be there when she gets settled, but will only be there to greet her."

He agreed. It was too soon for Max to leave the nest just yet. I drove home, and on the way I called my Dad to come help me carry the puppies inside.

He said he would be there waiting when I got home. To my surprise, the whole family was there, because they each wanted to hold a puppy and carry them inside. It was good to have my family help me.

On the days while waiting for my dogs to come home, I had made a special place in a corner of the sunroom because it was nice and warm there and no carpet. This way I could put newspaper on the wood floor, since the pups were so little yet. I also had an oversized bed for Sparkle to feed her young.

My family really fell in love with these cute puppies, and it was hard for them to pull away before they left. Then I let Max in and he sniffed each puppy, because these were his first offspring, then he went in the living room and lay down to take a nap.

The pups were all snuggled in with their mama and suckled her, then went to sleep. This was a wonderful sight to see. I went in the living room and also laid down for a nap, after getting a snack, because I was supposed to eat more than just three meals a day. Then I fell asleep.

When I woke up, I went outside to the mailbox to check on the mail and saw a lot of it. I brought it all inside and put it on the kitchen table, then fixed lunch. All went well the rest of the day and the week, and soon it was Friday afternoon, and after the duties were done, I made sure that Sparkle went outside for a bit and then brought her in and kept Max out to run and play while she was gone.

Next, I got into my truck and drove off to the small airport to pick up Sara. The plane was just landing when I arrived, and I waited for it to stop and unload, and then Sara was walking to the terminal and just had one small suitcase and a carry-on.

When she came inside, we gave each other a hug and then walked to the car. I put the suitcase in the back as well as the carry-on, and Sara got inside the truck and we put on our seat belts.

We drove toward home. When we got there, Sara said, "Your cottage is just like the one in my dream, but there is a small difference, for you have a larger area than the one in my dream."

After we put the luggage inside the extra bedroom, we both sat down at the kitchen table. I said, "When you had your dream, did the lady at the door of the cottage ever tell you her name?"

She said, "No."

I then said, "I just now got a short message from another guide of mine and I asked her if she knew the name, and she said the name is Ineldah. Does this help you any?"

Sara said, "No, but it may later."

Soon it was time for supper, and then afterwards, when all was cleaned up in the kitchen, we went to the living room. I let Max and Sparkle inside and asked Sara if she would like to see the puppies.

Sara said, "Yes," so we went to the sunroom to look at them. Sara said, "Oh my, they are so cute! I love this mixture of the two different breeds. I get a series of books called *Sparrow Island*, and in the story, the crippled sister had this mixed breed of dog and it makes for a very good service dog. When I get moved in, if you like, you can borrow my books and read them."

I said, "I would like that very much, because I like to read too."

After a while, we let the dogs out one more time before going to bed. As we were going up, I said, "I need to have a large doggie door made, so my dogs can go out when they need to. The only problem is the raccoons may try to come in, but it's a good thought, anyway."

We both slept well. We had a hearty breakfast and Sara helped me clean up. Then we went up the stairs and got dressed to go for a walk and take a look at the cottage. When we were ready, we were both on our way.

For some reason it did not take as long to arrive at the cottage. This was good. I saw some cars there and a gardening crew was there to do their work. They were soon done with this because this was the last day of their work. The crew left us and we went inside the cottage. Then I said, "I guess this is your first time to see the inside of the cottage you dreamed about, isn't it?"

Sara said, "Yes, it is, for I was on the outside talking to Ineldah in my dream. I noticed that it was very much the same as you live in, but it had more of the look, and this may sound strange, but what it was like in the cartoon of *Snow White and the Seven Dwarfs'* home, but a little more modern than that." All in all, Sara loved it and knew this was going to be a wonderful place to live in.

I asked if we could go outside and see if we could find the boat that was in her dream. "Did it look something like the shape of a pea pod?"

Sara said, "Yes, that would be fun."

Off we went, around the back, and found a small shed that was like a boat house that faced the river that circled the cottage and then went straight.

I said, "Shall we open the door and see what is inside?"

"Let's do just that."

We opened it and there was a canoe shaped like a peapod. "Wow, how neat is this?"

After that, we had to go back. While we walked, I asked her what she thought about the cottage. Sara said, "I can hardly wait to get moved in. I will be leaving tomorrow, which is Sunday, so I better get some things done in town today, before I have to go."

So we went to town in the golf cart. First, we went to the post office and then got the phone numbers of the lights and water and gas and other things, and then went to the diner to have lunch. Sara liked Cindy right off, and knew somehow that she was awake to things like she was. So the three of us had a nice visit on Cindy's coffee break.

Then we left and went to the bakery and got some goodies for supper and breakfast, and then went home to my cottage and enjoyed one another's company until way after supper time, and then Sara said, "I may be here sooner than three weeks because I, too, know this new place is my home, because it feels good to me."

Then we both went to bed. Thank goodness she had seen a bedroom downstairs at the cottage for her mother. What a relief that was for Sara.

The next morning we were both up early and had our breakfast and we walked around in the garden and the barn. Then it was time to leave to take Sara to the airport. It was not long after we arrived that Sara's small plane arrived and was ready to go. So we hugged and said we would see each other in two weeks, then off Sara flew.

When I arrived home, I brought Max in the house, then had lunch and laid down for a nap.

When Sara got home, she told her mother about the cottage and said it was perfect for the two of them. As she was talking, she asked her mom, "Are you still up to moving?" For Sara was. Her mom said she was, for this place was really getting in bad shape and they needed a safer place to live. She also said that she, too, had always wanted to live in a cottage with all the little bridges and little rivers running through the yard and all of the flowers.

Then Sara told her mom about the puppies. Her mom then said, "Oh my, I would love to see them when we get there, for I love that breed of dog."

Soon afterwards, Sara and her mother were tired, and for the rest of the day they laid down for a nap.

The next two weeks for them was very busy, with calling the Social Security office to make sure their checks were deposited in the bank in this new town, and changing banks to Bank One. Then they called the utility companies, to let them know the day they would be moving, and to give them the address where to send the last bill, and so on and so forth. They were busy packing items that were special and getting rid of things that they really should have gotten rid of a long time ago. It was not an easy task, but it had to be done. Some things they would leave behind, and if they needed them, they could get them later.

Two days before they were to leave, the big moving van came and started moving everything into the large truck. It took awhile because there was a lot of stuff. The truck left before they did, so Sara and her mother hired someone to drive them and their pets to their new home. They would probably get there before the moving company.

I offered the mini cottage for them to stay in until the truck arrived. In the meantime, the enclosed yard was fixed for Amberli to play in, located in back of the mini cottage. I had someone put twin beds in the cottage for Sara and her mother to use until the big moving truck had everything moved into their new cottage.

The big day came and went, and the townspeople helped too, so that Sara and her mom could move in. They were so happy to finally be able to live in their own place at long last, and they thanked me for my help, as well as everyone else. There was even a place to store the Rascal and other scooter.

Sara's mother used it to go over to the new place, and she used the walker to go inside the cottage. When Waneta saw the inside of the cottage, she began to cry with joy, but had to sit down because she was tired. All of this moving was hard on her, so Sara fixed lunch, and then her mom wanted to go to her room and take a nap.

Sara came to my cottage and got Amberli and the birds and brought them to the new home. Amberli loved her new home, too, and wanted to go outside, so Sara let her out in the new fenced yard just for Amberli, because she loved to run and there was a big running place for her.

After she did this, it was Sara's turn to relax. Then things went on for them as always, and this gave them a chance to get used to their new surroundings.

Meanwhile at my cottage ... It was the month of April and I had a chance to get to know a lot about my three cows and goats, because I was being taught how to take care of them as well as the chickens. There were not any eggs yet, so I had to keep buying them at the store until my chickens started laying eggs. There was a variety of different chickens that laid different colors of eggs, so it was going to be fun to bring them into the house when they were ready.

I learned that all three cows were going to have calves soon. This was very exciting. This was also true with the female goats. Somehow it helps the cows to have more milk when they give birth, as well as the goats.

One day during the month of April, the Native American people drove into my yard with a horse trailer and I saw them and went outside to greet them. They got out and opened the back of the trailer and placed a ramp to bring the beautiful horse to the barn. When I saw this horse, I was enchanted because she was so beautiful. This horse was white with many dark spots on the rump. Her name was Many Stars. She was also a tall horse.

Then, after admiring her, the Cherokee people led her to the barn and placed her in the stall. It's a very good thing that I had a large pasture for the cows and a horse now because I sure needed this. The people then told her that they would be back in a few weeks to give her the best idea on what to do in the meantime. They also said they would be by to help set up the herb garden.

Then off they went. I went into the barn and just stood there petting my horse and talking to her. I knew I was going to be very busy with all of this, but I was taking better care of myself now after the doctor gave me better medicine. I also was eating better and resting more.

I looked at Many Stars and noticed that her tummy was big and when I put my hand on it, something kicked. Then I said, "Oh my. You, too, are going to have an offspring."

So the next day I had the vet, Skip, come out and check on my horse. He said that she was nearly ready to give birth and it may be twins. I thanked him for coming out, and he said he had never delivered twin horses before. He said, "May I come out when it's her time?"

I said, "Of course, by all means, because this is all new to me as well." Then he left.

I was so excited that I called my father and told him the news, and he said, "Can I come out and see her?"

I said, "Yes, you can. Not only do I have a horse ready to give birth, but not long from now all three cows and some of my goats. This is very exciting for me, as you can tell."

My father has just gotten some horses a week or so ago, and a few of his, too, were going to give birth. This meant that his stables would be well on the way — a very nice business for him, for the riding stables and also the carriage-ride business.

When he arrived again, the whole family was there and they all went out to the barn to take a look at my first horse. They were awestruck when they saw how beautiful she was. My father said, "Yes, she has two very active ones inside. I, too, want to be here when they are born. I think it will be another two weeks when these little ones are born. I will come out, and also, when they are big enough, train them for you. Would you like this?"

I said I would. They all looked at the cows, too, and said it seemed that this was the year for twins because every one of these cows had very active young ones inside of them. They laughed and said, "You are on your way to having a herd of cows."

Then they looked at the goats and three of them were having twins, too. "We may have to build a bigger pen for all of them, and a milking mini stall just for your goat business. Well, we must go now, and thank you, we also have a surprise for you."

I then asked, "What is it?"

My father said that my brother was coming to town and wanted to know if he and his wife could live in the mini cottage in July.

I said, "This is great, because I know I can't do this all by myself. I was thinking, too, I may have to hire some men to help me here."

Then my father said that my brother's sons would be coming too.

Then I said, "After all the weddings, I will have plenty of space for them in the loft of the barn because of the three rooms the townspeople built for me. There is a bathroom for them. Everything is coming together rather nicely, and it's rather a shock, but it's okay because this has been my dream for a long time now. I had better see if I have enough property to build a bunkhouse as well as a special kitchen and dinning area to feed everyone."

Then my father said, "I think you have plenty of room for everyone as well as an area to make a big kitchen, but you really don't need a bunkhouse."

I thanked my dad and hugged them all as they left, and said, "I better go and take a nap. This has been a very exciting day for me."

I went inside my cottage and took my nap. A voice said to me, "Child, remember, you must have time to be alone for your health. This is why I have sent help your way. You need to continue your walks, and your spiritual work and training. So this is why we want you to take your walks because there is a nice place in the woods beyond the redwood trees after you cross the rope bridge. It's a place just above the rapids with a waterfall to the right that you, as well as Sara, can go and be alone, because Sara has to have a place to get away for an hour or two three times a week, being she takes care of her mother. Her mother does not have much longer on Earth because she, too, is being called home. So on Saturday, you and Sara must take a walk together to find the little hut. I have to go now, child, but remember, to take care of yourselves, and I will speak to Sara of this, too. For she needs to take better care of her health as well. We will talk again soon. Love and hugs, Yahweh."

I went about what I had to do after my nap. Soon it was night time again and time for bed.

The last two weeks of the month of April went fast and then it was two days before the wedding of my friend Jill at the bookstore. The preparations were being made ahead of time, so that had to be done at the restaurant so they could supply the food for the reception.

The day before the wedding, the garden was made ready with the arch with flowers and a pathway for the bride to walk on, and chairs set up. Now all we had to do was pray it would be a nice sunny day for the wedding.

The day of the wedding was nice, and the sun was out and no clouds in the sky. The barn was set up with rented tables and chairs, etc. The cake was delivered early and the food as well. This part was being set up. It was so beautiful how everything was being arranged. The bridesmaids and ushers were local as well. They didn't need to use the attic or the rooms in the barn in the hayloft.

Soon the guests were arriving and everyone was escorted to their proper places on each side of the aisle, and then it was time for the bride and her father to walk down the aisle, and, oh, yes, the groom was where he was supposed to be.

Soon the music started, and Jill and her father came down the aisle. They both exchanged personal vows to one another, and then were pronounced husband and wife. Then everyone clapped for the bride and groom, and they walked out of the garden and into the barn for the reception.

You could smell the fragrance of the barbecue and my stomach began to growl. This was starting to be a lot of fun after the guests greeted and gave the bride and grooms their best wishes. Then the best man gave a toast, and afterwards everyone was getting into a party mood. The country-western band played and some got up and danced after the bride and groom had their first dance, and the father of the bride had a dance with his daughter.

Then it was time to cut the wedding cake, and that cake was so beautiful with all the white flowers all done in frosting with green leaves. The couple gave each other a bite of cake. They had fun.

Soon it was time for them to leave because they had to get up early to catch a plane to Ireland for their honeymoon. First, the groom took the garter off his bride's leg and tossed it to the single young men, and then it was the bride's turn to toss her bouquet to the single women. This was a very pleasant wedding, and it was comfortable and not strained as some weddings are.

It was all over now, and the big clean-up could wait until tomorrow. Everyone left, and the parents on both sides took all the wedding gifts with them to keep until the couple came home from their honeymoon. The top of the cake was taken as well. The other part of the cake was gone, so I went into my cottage and upstairs because it was dark now, and brought Max in first, and then went to bed.

It had been a long day for everyone. I fell fast asleep after changing into my nightclothes and getting into bed.

I slept in the next morning, and didn't even hear the clean-up crew outside. That was nice, for I was still very tired, but I had to let Max out because he came and nudged me to get up. Thank goodness the cleaning crew was early, because shortly after that they were gone.

It began to sprinkle, so I brought Max inside. I made a fresh pot of coffee and just sat there for a while and looked out the window. When the coffee was done, I had a cup, then fed Max. He was a patient dog and so loving.

Then I noticed something about him. He was not as chipper as normal. He lay down and it didn't feel right, so I called Skip and told him about Max, how Max was lagging, and he said Max always had his shots each month. I should bring him in on Monday if he isn't any better.

I hung up the phone. Now I was really worried because I'd lost my friend, and now if Max did not feel any better, maybe I'd lose him too. Then I started to cry and some of it was from doing too much the past few days.

I then said to myself, "I have got to stop thinking this way, Max is just fine." So I ate my breakfast and went upstairs and got dressed. The animals needed to be taken care of.

When I arrived at the barn to check the cows, to my surprise I saw six calves, two of each standing with their mothers suckling milk. This was so sweet, and they were so cute. Then the little ones lay down and took a nap.

I checked on my horse, Many Stars, and she was doing fine — no babies yet. Then I fed the mother cows and the horse, and checked on the goats and fed them. I had another surprise: There were several kids feeding and getting used to standing. All of this warmed my heart and gave me joy. They were fed, and next I checked on the chickens and looked to see if there were any eggs yet. There were only about six of them, so I gathered them up in a basket, set them aside, and fed the chickens, then went back to the cottage, put the eggs away, and had another cup of coffee.

Next, I went to the living room and sat in the chair and relaxed. The rain started to come down harder, and I was glad that I got back inside when I did. I had to fix a fire in the fireplace because the rain was making it a little chilly. There was a damp feeling in the air. I got cozy with a blanket. This was Saturday and I decided to just stay home on Sunday because I was feeling a little under the weather.

The weekend went by fast and on Monday Max was still not doing very well, so after all was taken care of, I took Max to the animal hospital to get him checked over. After Skip did all of the tests, he told me that Max had cancer and would not be around very long.

I said, "This is strange because he seemed to be fine and lively when he played outside."

Skip said, "He may not have felt very well for a while. Remember how he acted when your friend passed on? That was not all emotional pain. It was something else."

I felt very sad and asked what I should do for Max.

Skip said," Just make him as comfortable as you can, but don't baby him because he needs to walk around and be outside. Let his passing be as natural as can be, but here are some pills you can put in his food to help him feel better."

I thanked Skip and took Max and left. As I was driving home, I told him, "Well, young man, you are going to have a pampering. You deserve this with all you have done to help by doing your part. If it was not for you, seven more female golden retrievers would not be going to have puppies now. So you have done a wonderful job."

Max looked at me and saw tears in my eyes, and even he had tears in his eyes.

When we got home, I made him comfortable after letting him outside and then bringing both Sparkle in, too. Then I left to go to town, to buy three steaks — one for Sparkle and one for Max and the other for myself — for I felt that I needed them to help us feel better.

When I got back and put the food away, I went out to the barn to check on Many Stars. She was still okay, but there was tenseness when I put my hand on her belly. Then a voice said, "You better call the vet and your father because your horse is in the beginning parts of labor."

I thanked the voice and went to the cottage to call Skip. He told me to just wait, because it was the early stages, "but have your dad come over just in case. If there is a change, call me right away."

I called my dad and he came right over to do what he could do to help. When he arrived, he went straight to the barn to be with Many Stars. He knew what to do until the vet would come, since his own horses had just given birth the other day. This horse was new to giving birth because it was her first. Many Stars began to whinny and so he got a rein and walked her, to help her feel better because this makes the pain not so intense.

I helped, too, and then he saw that the opening was beginning to show, that these little ones wanted to be born. I called Skip, and soon he was there after the call, for he must have driven at neck-breaking speed.

He parked his van and went to the barn. The first baby was coming feet first, so he and my dad worked feverishly to turn the baby horse around, and then the baby horse finally came out. It was a red-colored horse and a male. Soon the other baby horse came out and it was female. It was the same color as the mama.

They stood up on wobbly legs and went over to their mama to suckle. Then they both took a nap.

"Wow, that was awesome to see those two born today," Skip said. "I am so happy that they are both alive and well. Do you have a name for them?"

"I shall call the female Moon Beam and the male Wildfire."

Skip said, "Those are Native American names, aren't they?"

I said yes.

My dad said he would be getting back to the farm, but would be back tomorrow and would bring the family to see all the new young animals I had now. "And your brother Mike and his wife Martha are already here and will stay with us until after the June wedding for your friend Mandy."

I gave Dad a hug and was glad that help was on the way. Then, Skip said he had to get back as well. This was truly a very busy morning for all of us. Then I let Sparkle out, and then in, and then took a nap. I was pooped from all the excitement of Many Stars giving birth to her twins.

After my nap, I got busy cooking supper because this was a celebration as well as a treat for my dogs and myself. The steaks were cooled so they would not be too hot for Sparkle and Max. Then I cut them to get the bone off and fed them, and then I ate my supper.

Then we went up to bed and Max laid on the rug. I fell asleep in no time. The rest of the month was very eventful because of the cute ways the newborn animals were running and playing and having a good time getting used to just about everything. It was so heart-warming to watch them. It was much like watching children at recess at school, exploring and getting into mischief.

The Cherokee people came by one morning and helped me design the herb garden and brought herbs that I had never seen before. When it was all done, it looked fantastic. They also brought sage for me to burn. This was used to purify oneself as well as your home and other places. Then they wanted to see the baby horses, and when they saw the one with the red-like coat, they said this one should have a different name.

"Call him Phoenix because of being born feet first and almost not making it into this world." And so this was the new name for the red horse. Soon we were looking at the female horse and they said, "She, too, needs a new name, and since her spots are a brownish gold, call her Moon Stars, for she will birth special horses."

Then we said our goodbyes and, just before leaving, they said to bring Sara and Waneta by the reservation for a blessing because they were both of the stars and the mother would be leaving soon to go home. "Her mate is waiting for her, and still has more to do on the Other Side. With this ceremony, this will help to awaken her to who she really is. Sara has many powers to help planet Earth and is already doing work with her sister on the Other Side from the star system. She is your teacher and guide as well as to many others."

After they left, I called Sara and told her what was said, and Sara said, "You know what? Last night I had a dream about this. This is so wonderful."

Then I said, "Would you like to take a walk on Saturday?"

"Yes, I would," Sara said.

"I will see you then, and have a wonderful day," I told her.

Then Sara said, "I forgot to mention, I am going to plant a field of different kinds of lavender, and also wildflowers in the back of my property, as well as herbs."

"What will they be used for?"

"These will be used to help heal people's sickness, for I, too, am a Medicine Woman, Mary. This is going to be good to work together as a team and give lessons to help those that need help. Well, goodbye now, see you later."

The week went by fast and it was now already Saturday. I took care of the animals and fed all of them, then put them both out, and then fixed and ate breakfast and put snacks and water in my backpack.

Meanwhile, Sara was doing the same at her place. We both were on our way for a nice walk, and we walked on the rope bridge and through the grove of redwood trees. Then I said, "Oh look over there."

We saw a small building that was partly enclosed with a roof and the part right above the rapids was like a porch with a railing so that you would not fall when sitting on the porch dangling your feet in the water. "Let's go check it out."

So we did and climbed into it and up the steps by holding onto a rope railing of sorts. We took off our back backpacks and sat down to enjoy the sound of the water.. Soon we were in a deep meditative state and we could see our guides and talk to them each in a private manner of what we were both to do to help people who needed help, as well as mankind.

Soon we awoke to the present and a voice spoke to us, saying, "I am the spirit of water, earth, wind, and fire. Sara, you already know your special name, and what you came to Earth to do. Mary, you will soon know of your special name as well. These waters are healing waters, for mind and spirit, and when you both come here as often as time allows. This is a place of rest for your busy life on your many farms. Sara, we will send a horse soon to you, her name is Ginger, and a little pony to your mother that is strong enough to pull a small carriage with your mother in the carriage. It is a cute miniature horse that your mother has been wanting and this will make her last days enjoyable for her. This pony will be named Justice, and her coat is a very light tan color, into white, and the mane and tail are a darker tan color. Now relax and enjoy this special place that was meant not only for the two of you but also for Cindy. Farewell now. We will talk again soon."

We spent the rest of the time in silence and dangled our feet in the water. That felt so good to us. When we were done, we got up and dried our feet, ate our lunch, then packed up our backpacks, put them on, and headed home. This was a beautiful day's walk for the two of us. It made us feel more rested. Sara had a heart problem that didn't happen until the age of 71, and she had to slow down now. She had to eat more than one meal a day and get a lot of rest, or it would make her sick.

When we got home, we went our different ways, and when we got to our cottage, we put everything away and just enjoyed the rest of the day.

When Sara got home, the mail was in the box already, so she took it inside. Before looking through the mail, she saw to her mom's needs and made some tea and took the tray to her in the living room. There was tea and a snack on the tray, and she did the same for herself. Then she went through the mail and got rid of the junk mail. There were two letters addressed to her mother and she had a few as well.

There was one from her son. She opened it first because he didn't write very often to her through the years, and this was a treat to hear from him. He was married and lived in Houma, Louisiana. A few years back a terrible hurricane hit the area and a lot of people lost their homes and their lives.

Back to the letter: It said.

"Dear Mom:

"I could not take it anymore with my wife, and so we are separated for a while. Don't worry. I am still helping her, but there is just something missing. If I knew it would work, I would seek the help of someone to resolve our problems, but my funds are not that much, so it's best to leave this town and move to a place I can be in peace and get to know more of who I am.

"Mom, are there any jobs where you moved to? For I will need to work to support my wife and stepdaughters, but thank goodness one of them just got married and is no longer living at home. The younger one wants to stay with me when I get settled, because she wants a better life than what she has in Houma. If her mother agrees, then she can stay here when I move. She is very bright and will go places. I know the schools are better up there and just maybe this will do her good.

"I am waiting to see what she has to say. I have got to go now, but am living in a small apartment and I go off shore soon, so that's it, Mom.

"Let me know soon ok?

"Love J. P."

After reading the letter, Sara got up and made a call to her son, since the phone number was in the letter. It rang three times and her son answered.

"Oh! Mom, hi, how are you? I just woke up from a nap. It's good to hear from you. I just sent the letter seven days ago. And already you are calling."

Sara said, "There is not too much work here. But I sure could use some help. And like my friend across the street, I have a two-bedroom cottage you can live in if you like, and it's really cozy. Have you heard any more from your wife, and what your wife decided as far as her daughter coming out here to live with you?"

He said, "Yes, but she was not very pleasant about it, for she was in one of her moods."

"Well, son, you have to remember that Heather is her daughter after all."

"Yes, you are right, Mom."

"How would you like to stay here and help me?"

Her son said, "I would love it, because I have not seen you in over 30 years. Is it all right to come out now?"

Sara said, "Of course you can come now. You will love it here just as I do, and I have a barn too, and if you like, later we can get some horses to keep and ride. How does that sound to you?"

"That sounds wonderful. How is Grandma doing?"

"She is doing better since we moved here. J.P., when do you think you and your stepdaughter can move out here?"

"Mom, maybe in two weeks, because I need to give notice at my job and also where I live, so I have to fill out the change-of-address card. I don't have a bank account, so I am okay."

"What about your stepdaughter? Can you have her mom give you her school records and birth certificate?"

J.P. said, "Yes, that's all been done, because the stepdaughter is already here. She came over and said, 'I am sorry for moving in on you, but was so excited when Mom said it would be a better life for me that I could not wait any longer, so she said okay, you can go now.' We will both be on our way in two weeks or less."

"That's good, since you don't have furniture that works out fine. The little cottage already has furniture in it and I will have someone clean it real nice before you arrive."

"Mom, I will call you back on Monday and let you know how things are going. Bye, Mom. I love you."

It was Monday before Sara knew it, and in the late afternoon as she was outside in back, she heard the phone ring. She went inside to see who it was. When she picked up the phone, it was her son.

"Mom, you will never believe this in a hundred years. My boss said I don't need to give notice because they hired an extra crew, and so we are leaving tonight, and the landlady said I didn't have to leave a notice either because a young man was asking about a place to live. Mom, I can tell you, we are both so excited about the trip to where you live, and I have enough saved where we can visit some places in Arizona and also the Redwoods in upper California. Bye, Mom, I am so excited that I am going to pack my van now and be on our way. See you in a week or so. I love you, Mom, and so does Heather."

Sara knew she had better get busy and have someone come in and clean the cottage. Then she had to check on the school tomorrow for Heather, since she was in high school now. She decided to do this in the morning because she needed to take care of her mother's needs and start supper.

CHAPTER 7

MEANWHILE — AT MY cottage — I was getting things ready for the wedding on June 1st and only had two more weeks. Suddenly I remembered that Sunday was Mother's Day and I was supposed to give a short talk.

Then a new voice said: "Child, this is Mother Mary talking to you now. This is a very special day coming up tomorrow for all mothers. Talk from your heart, because this is the best way to do. So have courage, and know that you will be just fine. I will be in touch again soon."

I was most surprised to hear from the Holy Mother Mary. I said, "She is right, I can do this."

The rest of the day I worked on my potluck meals, because I had not done so in a while. On Sunday morning, I packed everything in the ice chest and put it all in the truck after the morning duties. The dogs had been out already. Then I drove to the chapel.

Sara had another ride from Grace because her car was bigger and able to take Sara and her mother. Sara and her mother sat in back, in case something happened.

Grace got up and gave a nice talk for mothers and said that it was a full-time job for all mothers because they were at home all the time, doing more than we may all know, and this is why mothers should be respected every day, and not just once a year.

It was my turn to talk:

"There are many mothers in the world. Most are two-legged ones, and the others either fly, or swim, or crawl, or walk on all four limbs, but they are still mothers of a different kind, because they love their young as humans do.

"I was watching the new mothers that have just given birth at my mini farm. If you could just see how endearing this is for them, you would just be enamored. They would never stop doing what they do with their young, even after they play. They are grazing in the field, and when the young are through with play, they come to mama for comfort. Then after they have their mother's milk, they lay down for a nap to dream. The mothers of four legs have it easy, you see. They are just there for their young, don't you see?

"So, no matter what mother you may be, you are loved for your unending work from heaven to thee. All around you, don't you see? So, as you go about your daily duties, remember you are all being watched from heaven above, and comfort is there for each one of these. Enjoy your special day today. I love you all."

After I was done, there was silence, for this was a very different way of letting them know about the many types of mothers.

Grace spoke up again and gave a prayer, and then we all sang the last hymn, "Home can be a Heaven on Earth":

> *Home can be a heaven on earth.*
> *When we are filled with love,*
> *bringing happiness and joy.*
> *Rich blessings from above.*
> *Warmth and kindness, charity.*
> *Safety and security.*
> *Making home apart of heaven,*
> *Where we want to be.*

When the hymn was done, we gathered and went outside and hugged one another before going to the potluck.

After we all arrived at the farm of George and Georgia, and placed our food on the different tables, we formed a circle and said a blessing before eating. Then we formed a long line and we each picked up a plate and began serving ourselves the food we wanted. Of course, Sara had her mother sit down because she had a hard time standing. So Sara went and got her mother's food to eat, and some elderly ladies came and sat with Sara's mother and were having a nice talk as they ate.

Then the ladies invited her mother to join them at their different homes, so that Sara's mother could have some new friends. This was good for her. Waneta did not have this when they were in her hometown of Ventura. It seemed that after her stroke, when she was not able to drive any more, they just stopped coming to visit her. Waneta was so happy to meet new friends and — the best part was — they would come and pick her up when they had a meeting each month.

After all had eaten, everything was cleaned up. Sara's mother was taken to the car, and Sara walked behind, carrying the dishes to place in the trunk of the car. Then Grace drove them home to their cottage while Sara made a couple trips to the car to bring everything inside. They hugged and said goodbye and Grace left to go home.

After this, Sara helped her mother go to her bed, so she could take a nap. Then she let Amberli inside and she, too, lay down and took a nap. As Waneta was about to fall asleep, she said a prayer of thanks for a wonderful Sunday and she knew that at long last she would no longer be lonely. This nice town had some good people in it.

Then she fell asleep. In the evening the phone rang. As Sara picked up the phone, she heard her son's voice. He said, "Hello. Happy Mother's Day, Mom."

Sara said, "Why, thank you. Where are you now?"

He said, "We are in Ventura, and I called to ask if there is anything you would like us to bring from the old house that you were not able to bring with you?"

Sara said, "Yes, there is," and gave a list to him. "Oh yes, I left a key on a nail just inside the garage door, in case of an emergency, so you can use that."

Then he said, "There is still fruit on the plum trees. I will see if you left an ice chest behind and fill it with ice from the store. Would you like that?"

Sara said, "Yes, I would like that. Where are you headed now?"

Then J.P. said, "We will stay at a motel tonight, but early in the morning we will drive as much as we can toward the redwood area to see them — the reason being — Heather has never seen this. Oh

Mom, I forgot to mention, we went to Disneyland a few days ago, and Heather and I had a lot of fun. Well, I have to go now, Mom, so I can put the things you need in the back of my truck, and then pick some plums. Heather will help me. So, see you in a couple days, Mom."

Then Sara said, "When you left Houma, Louisiana, did you — or were you — able to take your personal keepsakes with you, like baby pictures that I gave you?"

He said, "I made sure of that and didn't leave them behind."

"Well, you be careful now driving the rest of the way up here."

"I will, Mom. Oh, before I hang up, can I talk to Grandma?"

"Sure you can." Sara handed the telephone to her mother.

"Hi, Grandma. Happy Mother's Day. How are you feeling now?"

She said, "I am so much happier up here than I was in Ventura. I met some new friends today and they are going to include me in their monthly meetings."

J.P. said, "That's great. You take care now, and we will hopefully be there in two days or so. Goodbye, Grandma, and tell Mom goodbye for me, okay?"

"Yes I will, and we love the two of you."

After they got off the cell phone, he and Heather got busy and picked the plums, put them in the ice chest with ice. They next went to the nearby motel and got in their twin beds and went to sleep, because they wanted an early start in the morning.

They got up at 5:00 AM, got dressed and loaded up their suitcases, and were on their way. They first stopped at Denny's for breakfast, then left and drove the long drive they had planned, with a stopover in Salvang because he wanted to bring Mom a treat of candy that she loved so much — it was Divinity. Heather loved this place; they tried a lot of goodies while there, and then were on their way once again.

In Oregon, a lot of activity was going on. Sara and her mom, Waneta, decided to ride their scooters into town, because they had some errands to do together. Waneta was very happy about this, for it was the first time she got to see the town.

Sara asked about the school for her step-granddaughter and was shown where to go in early August to register. School didn't let out until the middle of June.

Waneta loved this small town right away, for it was an easy town to get to and had lots of ramps for her Rascal that she had to get around in.

As soon as all the errands were done, they went to the diner to have lunch. They saw me there. Cindy made a place for Waneta to sit, and Sara sat down next to me and we ordered. Waneta had a sandwich called a Reuben and Sara had a Monte Cristo. I had Pita bread with tuna salad, and we all had iced tea.

This was so much fun for us. Cindy had a break just after serving our lunch. There were introductions all around, and it was like kindred spirits all joined together. This was a very joyful day for all of us.

Sara said her son would be there in a couple days with his step-daughter, and they would be staying in the cottage in back of her home. "I can hardly wait, for I have not seen him in over 30 years."

I said, "That is a long time. How could you bear being away from him so long?"

Sara said it was not easy. It was not given for her son at the time. There was not enough money for the trip. Cindy and I said thought that was sad.

"Well, Mary, what do you have going on in the next two weeks?"

"My friend Mandy is coming to our town to get married on June 1st, and will be staying at the cottage until after the wedding. Then the new couple will move into their own place in a nice farmhouse with a wrap-around porch, not far from town. Mandy bought Jill's bookstore, and her new husband will be working at the animal hospital, and also doing jobs at helping the farmers alongside of Skip. It's a wonderful job for him."

"Cindy, I heard that you, too, are a Star Seed and are learning more each day," said Sara.

"Yes, I have," said Cindy, "I want to learn more."

Sara said, "I am a teacher of insights and I am going to be helping you to wake up."

Cindy said, "This is wonderful, for we have been waiting a long time for you to come and teach us."

"Oh I will call you and find out more this evening. I am so glad to meet you. I have to go back to work."

By this time, they were done eating and paid and left a tip for a wonderful lunch, and then Sara helped her mother outside to her Rascal, and she got in her scooter and left.

I left, too, and got into my golf cart and drove home.

When all of us got home, we noticed a lot of mail in our mail boxes and took it all inside. Sara also piled her mail in the basket of her scooter and she and her mom drove the rest of the way on the dirt road to their cottage. As they were leaving, they waved goodbye.

"Well," said Sara, "we sure have a lot of mail today."

Waneta said,"Yes, I noticed. I guess the political people will not hear from me, for enough is enough. I need a nap."

So, after they got inside, Waneta went to her room to lie down. Sara let Amberli inside and then went through all of the mail. Then she put away the scooters and plugged them in to recharge.

Meanwhile, at my place, I put away the golf cart and plugged it in, then went through the mail. Twenty minutes later, the phone rang.

When I answered, a tearful woman said, "Mary, this is Mandy. There isn't going to be a wedding after all."

I asked, "Why?"

Mandy said, "While my husband-to-be was working at the animal clinic, some person out of his head came in and was holding a gun. And as my husband-to-be was coming into the waiting room, this man with the gun started shooting, and one of the bullets struck him right in the head and he died right away."

I asked if anyone else was hurt, and Mandy said, "No."

"Do they know why this man was doing this?"

Mandy said, "This man used to work at the clinic, and he had gotten fired because they caught him stealing drugs from the cabinet."

"What happened after this man did the shooting?"

Mandy said, "He shot himself and died right there in the clinic."

I said, "Oh Mandy, I am so sorry for this. Are you still going to come anyway?"

"Later, after the funeral."

I said I understood. "Is there anything I can do now for you? For you have a week and a half before the wedding would have taken place."

Mandy said, "Would you cancel everything for me, as far as the chapel and cake and flowers, and the carriage ride, etc.?"

"Yes, I can do that for you."

"Have you told the bridesmaids and ushers yet?"

"Yes, I did."

"Well, you know what, Mandy? I will help you to get through this, as well as Sara. Sara will help as well. What about the house you were going to move into?"

Mandy said, "It was all paid for, and I will have to have a place to live, so I am keeping it."

Then I said, "You take as long as you like, because the book store will still be here when you are ready to move here. Oh, one last thing ... what about the honeymoon trip?"

Mandy, said, "I was able to book a different trip for later, after I am moved to your wonderful town."

"That's a good thing to know, because some of those places don't give your money back."

"That's right, and they didn't give my money back," Mandy said.

"Now, Mandy, you just take it slow, and my town will help you heal."

"Oh Mary, you are so kind to me, and I am so happy to have you as a friend. I must go now and I will be there when all of this is over."

"You are a valued friend of mine, too, and thank you for telling me ahead of time. We will have time to talk when you get moved here. Goodbye now."

We both hung up the phone, and I sat at the kitchen table, stunned by this tragic news. By now all chances of napping were gone, but now I knew I had to get supper started and feed all the animals before it got dark.

I made a small supper out of leftovers of what I had in the fridge, and then I went to the barn to feed all of the animals before I retired for the evening. When I came in, I ate my supper that was warming in the oven on low, and fed my dogs, and then went to the living room with an iced tea and sat on the sofa to take all of this in.

In the morning a lot of calls would have to be made, but for now I just sat and prayed for my friend Mandy, her husband-to-be, and the young man who had killed him as well as himself. I prayed for them all. I knew that Yahweh understands this man doing the shooting, since he is a loving God — that he was helping him on the Other Side.

Then Yahweh spoke to me: "Yes, my child, this kind of thing is forgiven, because his soul was deeply hurt, and the stealing at the clinic was his first offense, so he was not a criminal — just a mixed up soul. He will go to a temporary penal colony that deals with the lesser crimes on a distant planet. Since he was remorseful, he won't be there very long."

"I am so glad to hear this news, Yahweh, because sometimes we just don't *think* when we do things, and then we get ourselves into trouble. I say this because not a soul on Planet Earth can say they don't make mistakes. All of us make minor ones every day."

"This is true, my child. I must go now, for I have a lot of souls to take home, including the young husband-to-be. We will talk again soon."

"Thank you, Yahweh."

After this, Max and I went upstairs to bed, and the next morning I was up bright and early to do all of my chores. I had my own breakfast and fed the dogs, and then cleaned the kitchen.

When all was done, I sat down in the living room and started making all of the calls for Mandy, to cancel everything for her. After this was done, I called my father.

"Mary, what can I do for you?"

I then told him the story about Mandy, and then my father said, "Is she going to be all right?"

"I think so, Dad, but this loss will take awhile for her to get over. I just wanted you to tell my brother that he can move in any time he likes, for everything is still the same. There is a double bed in the cottage for him and his wife."

My father then said, "That's good. When they sold their home of many years, they also sold all of their furniture."

"If they like, Dad, I can get someone to enlarge the cottage for them."

Dad then said, "Do not worry about this, Mary. For I can help with this, and so can your brother later on, when they can make plans of how to design it."

"Then yes, I will."

"Bye, Mary, I have work to do. I will call you tonight and let you know what they say."

"Bye, Dad." I hung up the phone. I had to go to town and get some supplies for I was running low. I went upstairs and got dressed, then put the dogs out while I was gone.

This morning I decided to take the golf cart to town because it was very hot, and it was cooler to be in the golf cart with the canopy on top to shade me from the hot sun. I went to the animal hospital first, and said I forgot to call Skip and tell him about the young man — that this young man would not be there after all. Then I stopped and said, "So much is going on that I am getting confused. It was the husband-to-be of Mandy that was killed."

I went to the General Store and bought a bunch of food items, and it was a good thing I remembered to transfer the ice chest to the golf cart because of the cold items that I bought. Afterwards, I went to the hardware store to see Hank. I had not talked to him in a while. When I got there, he was really busy, so I decided to come another time. Next, I went to the library and talked to Grace and picked up some books.

Grace said, "I am so glad you stopped in, for I have some news for you."

"Yes, what is it, Grace?"

"Since Sara is here now, I have decided to set up some classes at the chapel so I can start teaching the aware ones at the church how to wake up to their full part of why they are here."

"That is wonderful, Grace, for I do know that all these wonderful souls that live in our town are here for a reason, and we're all called to come, and they heeded the call."

"Yes, that's true," said Grace, "and also I have a feeling who she truly is, and what part she has to play in the awakening."

"I feel this too," said I.

Grace said, "I called her this morning and asked if she could give a talk at church on the Sunday past Father's Day, and she agreed."

"Oh, I am so glad. The first Sunday I gave a talk, I realized they were so silent that they all got the call to be ready to start learning more, and also each one of them had their own private message from what I said to them."

"I could see and also feel it within my soul," Grace said.

I said, "I came also to check out some books, and then I am going to have lunch at the diner. Would you like to join me?"

"No, I just got a load of books and have to get them ready to put on the shelves, but someday sooner than you think I would like to come over and visit with you and take a walk."

"I would like that," I said, and then I left and went to the diner.

When I got there, I checked to see if the contents of the ice chest were all right. I had put dry ice in the chest for the frozen goods I had bought at the store. When all was checked on and was safe, I went into the diner.

Cindy was very excited for some reason, but did not say anything just yet because she had to wait for her coffee break. I sat at my favorite table and ordered a veggie burger, with the works, and iced tea. After Cindy brought my lunch, she sat down and was bursting to tell me the news.

I said, "Calm down, and take it slow, my dear."

Cindy said, "Last night it was very warm, so I took a walk in the country close to where I live. Well, anyway, I heard something of a kind of swishing sound. I looked up in the clear, star-lit sky and saw a spacecraft land nearby. As I watched, the door opened and a small creature got out. This creature was grey, and the eyes wrapped around the head. I think the creature was female. Then the creature spoke to me through telepathy and said, 'Have you met Sara?' I told her yes. Then she said, 'We are friends, and she is my adopted sister from eons ago, and I wanted to contact you and tell you, so you would know what I look like. I saw that it was time to do so, because you have no fear and are very aware.' "

"What did you say when she said this?"

"I was so excited and said, 'Welcome to you,' and 'I would like to learn more about you.' Soon the ET said, 'You will learn more soon. My name is Commander Sanni Ceto. I am reincarnated on your Earth and live in Arizona now. I am in a hybrid form. You will learn many things because you, Sara, will have a private session by the river in July. The date will be set up soon.' Then Commander Sanni Ceto got in her small craft that was shaped like a triangle, and flew off very fast."

"Thank you for telling me this," I said. "Yes, indeed, we will have a private meeting in July sometime, and we will have a new member to our group, for Grace is special too. I knew this the first time I met her. Well, I must go now, for I have frozen goods in the ice chest and I need to get them home into the freezer. Call me when you have time, and we will talk more about this. Bye now."

When I got home and put everything away, I felt that things were going at a faster pace than I was used to, as far as what was said today. I got a nice glass of iced tea, for it was hot outside, and went outside to the gazebo and sat in the shade to digest all of what was said today, and I knew that there was a good reason for all of it, and what better place for these things to come about than in this nice little town I now lived in? I was so happy I moved here, for I knew that the whole area was a melting pot of good things to come, as well as fantastic sights to see.

Then I thought it was so nice to sit in my own backyard and not be disturbed by city noise. I heard the phone ring just then and went to answer it. It was my brother, and he asked if he could move in today. I said that he sure could. "What time are you coming over?"

"I am on my way now."

"Oh, that's great. I will go and open the door so you can move in." Then I said goodbye and opened the cottage door.

Soon after this, my brother and his wife arrived and the moving in began, and I helped them. It didn't take long because they didn't have that much. Afterwards, I asked them what they would like for supper tonight, since it was their first night in their new cottage.

"Oh, no you don't, you are not going to cook for us," said my brother's wife. "It's my treat. When we are settled, I will start cooking and let you know when it's ready."

I said, "Thank you, for I was ready to take a nap."

The wife said, "Good for you. You have done enough today."

So I went inside and lay on the sofa and fell to sleep right away.

At Sara's cottage there was a lot going on as well, because she just had a call from her son J.P., and he said they would be there in an hour. So Sara opened the cottage door as well as windows to cool it off.

Then I went about making some sandwiches and put some tea glasses in the freezer to chill them, to make them even colder, and prepared watermelon for afterwards. Then her son drove up and got out and Sara went to greet them and gave them each a hug. She helped them carry their things, which she had her son to bring inside and put away, and helped them move their things into their cottage where they would be living.

After they went inside, Heather said, "I love this little cottage. It's so beautiful." Then Heather found the bedroom that would be hers and came running out with tears in her eyes and gave Sara a big hug. "Thank you, Grandma Sara, it's what I have always wanted."

Sara said, "I am so happy you like it."

Heather said, "I do, I do," and J.P. liked his room, too, and gave his mom another hug.

"Thanks, Mom."

"I guess the two of you are hungry. Come on over to my cottage so we can eat, for your grandma is hungry too." They said they would as soon as they hung up their clothes in the closet.

Soon they came into the kitchen and they all sat down at the table and praised God by holding hands, and then we ate.

They said, "You were right, Mom, we were hungry."

Sara asked Heather how she liked the trip out there, and she said, "I had the most wonderful time I had in my whole life."

"What did you like best?" asked Waneta.

"I liked the tall trees in the redwood forest. I have never seen trees like that, and from what I have seen of this town, it is so beautiful here."

"Yes, child, this is only the beginning of what your eyes will see," said Waneta.

Heather said, "I can hardly wait," and then Sara asked her son how he felt about everything so far.

He said, "I really love this place, and after we eat, I want to see the barn you told me about."

Sara said, "Yes, we will go there after we eat. Would you like some watermelon?"

"No, we are too excited to eat any more." So they helped Sara clean up the kitchen, and then went out the back door to the barn.

Sara's mom said, "I am tired and want to go lie down."

So J.P. helped her to her room. Then, after this, they all went outside and walked to the barn. When they got there, they looked inside and saw four stalls for horses and also a place for one cow if needed, because they didn't want too many animals. Then he said, "I see a great place for chickens, and I will build you a coop, Mom, for I know how to do this."

Sara said, "That would be wonderful, because I would sure like to have fresh eggs."

Her son said, "It will be done." Then he added, "The roof on the barn needs work. I will fix that next week for you, because when we get the animals, we don't want any leaks."

Then Heather said, "Oh my, look, Dad ... a swing. I love swings." Sure enough, hanging from the rafters of the barn was a swing.

"Well, I am tired, and I am going to take a nap," J.P. said.

"What about you, Heather, are you tired too?"

"I just want to take all of this in and stay outside for a while and just enjoy."

So everyone took a nap and Heather sat in the gazebo and daydreamed. She was tired, of course, but in a way this new life was really too much for a young mind to handle. She also felt like she was dreaming, and did not want the dream to end. But as Heather was sitting in the lounge chair, she, too, fell asleep in the gazebo.

Soon everyone was awake from their naps and it was late afternoon. Heather went to the cottage when she woke up and changed her clothes for the evening. J.P. was opening his things, sorting what he wanted to keep out and what he wanted to put away. Sara and her mother were in the kitchen, working at getting supper ready in their own cottage, and Amberli wanted outside again. All was nice and felt good for everyone.

There was a knock on the front door and Sara wondered who it could be at this hour. Then she opened the top door opening, to see who was there. An elderly man and woman stood outside.

"Hello," said the elderly man. "We have a cabin and property near the foothills, and we had to come down and meet you."

"That's not the whole reason we are here," said the elderly woman. "We are getting up in years and have some horses that are going to need a new home. We noticed that a young man is here now living in the other cottage."

Sara said, "Yes, come on in. We are getting supper ready. Would you like to have supper with us?"

"We will come in, but we can't stay long, and, no, we already ate our supper." They sat down to talk as Sara's son entered the room. Heather followed.

Sara said, "Here is the young man now. He is my son, J.P."

They all introduced one another and then the couple said, "Would you like to come over to our place tomorrow, so you can look at the horses? The reason is that we have to go in a week to be close to our children because they are going to be taking care of us."

"That is so nice that your children will be taking care of you, and very refreshing in these times," said Sara.

The couple said, "Anyway, we have a couple of nice horses, and one mini horse that some would call a pony, and the carriage to go with the pony. We don't need any money for them because we have enough to use for our later years. Would you like to have these horses?"

"Yes," they all said. "How did you know that we would be looking for some horses?"

The elderly couple said that they already knew about the family before they even moved here.

"What time would you like for me and my son and granddaughter to come over?"

The couple then said, "After lunch tomorrow. And one other thing: Our log cabin is right near the edge of a lake by the foothills. You probably didn't notice it when you and Mary took a walk one day. We are down the road in back of your cottage. We are hidden from view by the brush from the road. This is a lake that many like to put their boats on and go fishing. Oh, before we leave to go home this evening, our cabin will need some loving hands to watch over it, and we want you to be the loving hands, so we will talk more tomorrow. Bye now."

After the couple left, they all sat in the living room in silence because they were in shock. Soon they came to, and Sara and Heather went into the kitchen to get supper ready so they could all eat. When supper was ready, they didn't have much to say to one another. This was too much to handle in one day for them, but somehow they got through it, although something came to them.

"How did they get here? I didn't see their car. Did any of you?"

"No, we didn't."

Sara said, "This lake is three miles down the gravel road." This was truly a mystery. "Well, let's not try and solve it tonight. Does anyone want dessert?"

"Yes," they all said.

Sara brought in a peach pie with ice cream she made early in the day. After they ate, J.P. and Heather went to their cottage after hugging Mom and Grandma.

When they got to their own cottage, Heather took a shower and put her night clothes on, and then J.P. went in and did the same. They were both exhausted after the long day, so both fell sleep.

At my cottage:

There was a lot going on here, too. My brother Mike and his wife Martha soon called everyone to supper and we had a wonderful reunion together, talking about times. My brother mentioned that in a week or so his sons and their wives would be here as well.

The first son's name was Harry and the wife was named Tara. The second son's name was Fred and his wife's name was Freda.

"We know that you have rooms in the loft of the barn, but we want to know if it's all right with you later, if we build some cottages on the next property, which is for sale, and it would be great for my sons and their wives."

I said, "Sure. That sounds great." For I understood that they needed their own space while they worked here. "Yes, do please go ahead and buy the property."

"Thank you, sis, that is so understanding of you. We don't have any daughter and this will be just perfect."

Then all became silent. They had a lot of things to ponder for the upcoming weeks. We were all tired after I helped with the dishes and we all said goodnight and hugged, and then I went back to my cottage and let the dogs in and covered my birds and went to bed.

The next morning after I took a shower and put on clean clothes, I went downstairs and did what I always do in the morning, then sat down and drank a cup of coffee. Then I went to the barn and saw that my brother was already there, taking care of things. He was singing to himself when I got there, and I startled him a bit. I said, "I'm sorry. I should have called out first. I didn't know you were in here."

He said, "That's all right. I am just so happy to be here with you and close by our family. I started to milk the cows because they are full of milk. They are such sweet animals, and that's the reason why I am so happy. The young ones already had their milk, and I took them to the play yard. If they get any bigger, soon they will have to be separated, so there isn't any interbreeding with sisters and brothers. Right now they are okay."

I said, "Thank you. I didn't realize this. Should I have the vet sterilize them later? For I really don't want to part with them just yet. They can be used to breed other dairy cows."

While my brother was taking care of the cows and other things, I went to check on my horse, Many Stars, and said, "This is a nice day to take them out to the fenced pasture and let the mother run with her babies colts." I led the mother and her young to the pasture, and gave my horse a hug and let her run with her young.

Next, I checked the chickens to see if they had enough eggs. Sure enough, this time there were at least two dozen different colored eggs. What a joy to see this. I went inside and noticed that my brother's wife was in the garden weeding, and I said, "Good morning to you. How did you sleep last night?"

Martha said, "Very well. I just had to get out here, because I love to garden. Would you mind if I start a vegetable garden next spring, because I realize it's too late now to start a garden now."

I said, "Yes, I was thinking the same thing, but I've been so busy, I just didn't get around to it."

"Thank you, Mary. We can work together on this and it will be a lot of fun. I know you have a very nice herb garden started."

"Yes. My Cherokee friends are helping with this. We plan to harvest them when they are ready, and dry them in a shed. This is for cooking and for medicinal purposes as a natural way of healing."

"That's wonderful, Mary. Can I help with all of this?"

I said, "Yes, I would love to have all the help we can get. Oh, I better get these eggs in the kitchen, and there is enough here for you as well. My chickens are really starting to produce a lot of eggs now."

"Sure, I will be in later after I am done here."

I went into the kitchen with my eggs and set the basket on the counter. My brother and his wife came in and got the eggs and went to their cottage.

I called Skip and asked if I could bring Max in tomorrow and Skip said, "Yes. I was just going to ask how Max was doing."

"Good. I will see you tomorrow morning."

Soon my brother came in and said that he noticed that I had a nice machine to help homogenize and pasteurize milk in the barn. "Have you thought of what you want to do with all of this milk? For I also took care of milking the goats."

I said, "I am thinking of giving the milk to those who don't have much money to buy their milk, and even started a food bank off to one side of my property."

My brother said, "That is so nice of you, sis, to think of doing this, for we need to help out people more in this life."

I said, "I will call the General Store and tell them that if they know anyone who likes goat milk, we have our first batch."

My brother said, "We can make goat cheese and also cheese from the cow's milk. This is going to be work, but a lot of fun. One of my sons has learned about cheese making in college, so he can help with this."

I said, "This is going to be a very nice family operation with all of the talent we have."

My brother said, "Yes, indeed. I called the number of the person who owns the property next to yours, and they will be by this afternoon to talk to me, and it's 70 acres of good land. This will also be good to plant food for canning and other kinds of storing and to help the poor. And let's have the mini warehouse on the property."

I said, "That sounds wonderful. I just may take up basketry with the Cherokee people and blanket weaving, so we can have even more to help others. I wonder if your son's wives would like to get into this with me."

"Yes, they would."

"The rooms in the attic are set up. I plan to use these as sewing rooms, so the ladies from town can come and do quilting. Well, all this has made me tired and hungry just thinking about it," I said.

So he left to go to his cottage and have lunch.

That morning at Sara's place was busy with activity and a lot of excitement. Sara made pancakes and bacon on the side. And if they were still hungry, she would fix eggs. Even Waneta, Sara's mother, was extra chipper this morning. The breakfast went well and everyone was stuffed.

After they ate, Sara and her son went out to survey the barn, and to see how to use the land for the good of all. Sara told her son that she wanted to plant a field of different types of lavender to use for different things. She needed a special shed to dry them after it was harvested.

J.P. said, "I will build a place near where you plant, so you don't have to carry it so far, for I have time on my hands and like to stay busy. I better check the pasture fences, to see what shape they are in, since we will have horses soon to graze there. Yesterday I was looking at the inside of the barn, and you do have plenty of room for the seven large horses and the little pony. In back of the barn is a carriage house for the small carriage. Is there anyone you know in town that can help me with the barn roof?"

Sara said, "I will call the hardware store and ask."

He said, "I love you so much, and thanks so much for letting us live here. Heather and I love it here."

"We can spend the rest of our years here at long last, as a close mother and son. Do you ever have any dreams that you wanted to do with the rest of your life?"

"Yes, Mom, I have always wanted to be able to live in a nice place like this, and not have any more worry where I would be getting my next meal from, or a place that would not be destroyed by the weather."

Sara said, "Well, you do not have to ever worry anymore, for you are home now. I am so sorry that you and Stacy have broken up, for that was very hard on the both of you, not just you alone."

"Yes, Mom, it was, but soon I will be over it, and with you helping me through this, I will heal soon."

"Son, you are forgetting one thing, and that is that Stacy is also hurting. Think about this, okay? You both have things to work on."

"Okay, Mom."

Soon they had their lunch, and then J.P. drove his grandma and stepdaughter to the log cabin three miles away while Sara drove the Rascal. When they got there, they pulled onto the property and parked, and then J.P. helped his grandma out and fixed the wheelchair for her because it was too far for her to walk.

They greeted the couple and then they all went to the barn. All of them walked inside and saw all of the horses and fell in love at first sight. Sara's mom saw the pony and tears ran down her cheeks, so Sara said, "Are you all right, Mom?"

Waneta said, "Yes, I just love that little pony, for I have always wanted to hug one of them when we used to visit Salvang in California."

J.P. wheeled his grandma over to the pony and then brought the pony out so she could hug it. This was a sight Sara would never forget, and so she was glad she brought her camera. She took a picture of her mother hugging the pony. Then she saw the red color horse and she, too, began to tear up.

She went over to this horse to hug her, and then noticed the horse was bulging on both sides. She asked, "Is she about to give birth?"

The couple then said together, "Yes."

"Oh my, this is wonderful. This is going to be my horse and I already have a name for her."

"What is that?" they asked.

"Ginger. I will call her Ginger."

They all smiled, for they already knew this would happen. They did not say a word.

Then Heather saw a horse that caught her eye. This horse was a beautiful palomino and the color of beige. She, too, was going to give birth. Heather was so excited to see this horse. She had to go hug her, and she, too, cried tears of joy to finally have a horse of her own.

Then J.P. saw a male horse that was chestnut in color and he knew this was his horse. He said, "Mom, I have a name for him because of the star between his eyes."

"What will be his name?"

"Starlight."

They said to the couple that they indeed had plenty of room for all of the horses. Then the couple said to them, "All of them come with saddles and the works."

"When can we take them to our place?"

The couple said, "Anytime you like."

"We will be back, for we have to find a horse trailer to transport all of them."

"Not to worry, dear ones, we have one in the back of the barn, if you would like to first attach it to your truck."

J.P. said "Yes, I can do that. We will be back for it after taking the horses home."

"That's fine," said the couple.

Soon all of the horses were loaded onto the horse trailer and they drove them home to their own barn. Then, after J.P. settled the horses into the trailer, he looked back and noticed that the carriage also had a trailer hitch, so after he drove the horses to their new home, he drove back to the cabin and hitched the carriage to his truck. But before he left, he said to the couple, "Is there anything we can all do for you? Since you have given us all of these beautiful horses?"

They said no, because they knew they had given them to the right people. J.P. then said, "Thank you so much, and said goodbye."

As he drove home he had tears in his eyes for all of the loving feelings he had felt the past two days. Then he unhitched the carriage and put it away in the carriage house. He had a lot of work to do in the morning to fix the fence.

Early the next morning, J.P. fed the horses and gave them water. Then he went out to the pasture and saw that a couple fences needed repair, and since there was a temporary corral for the horses until the fence was fixed, he put the horses there so they could walk around and stretch their legs. Then he went back and had breakfast with his mom and grandma and Heather.

He said, "Mom, I may need some help with the fences. Does your friend Mary know anyone that can help?"

Sara said, "Yes, after breakfast I will call her, because her father is a horse farmer."

"Thanks, Mom, that will be a great deal of help. The horses will need a bigger place to exercise."

Sara called me and asked if my father could help her son in the pasture so that the horses that were given to them could have a larger area to run and play in.

"I will call Dad and see what he knows. You need to call Hank at the hardware store and get the supplies for the fences."

Sara said thanks to me and hung up. I then called my father and asked him about repairing the pasture fences, and if he was not able to do this, did he know anyone that could help Sara's son J.P. with this?

He said, "I can't do it this morning, but I will call and find someone and then call Sara and tell her who will be coming."

I said, "Thank you, Dad."

Sara called the hardware store and asked if he could have someone send some supplies for the pasture fencing this morning.

Hank said yes, he had just gotten a call asking if anyone could help her son J.P. with the fences. "I will be sending Jerry out, and he will help, for it's important that these horses have a place to run and graze. When everything is loaded, Jerry will be right over."

Sara said, "Thank you so much," and then hung up the phone. She then told her son that Jerry from the hardware store was loading up the supplies and would be over soon.

J.P. then said that after this was done he could let the horses out. "Thanks, Mom, for calling them for me."

Jerry drove up and asked where the repairs had to be made. Then he drove out in the truck. Luckily, there were only two or three places that had to be repaired, and with the two of them, they got the work done within two or three hours.

J.P. asked him if he knew of anyone to help build a chicken coop for his mom, and also to help repair the roof of the barn before the fall and winter rains and snow. Jerry said he did, and that would be he and some other men in the farming area.

J.P. thanked him, and Jerry said, "We could help with the chicken coop next week, and the barn roof in a month, because I have to gather a bunch of men together to come out and help."

J.P. said, "That is wonderful. It's fun working with you."

Jerry said he had to get back to the hardware store and would be in touch, but said, "In the meantime, you need to come in and get some supplies for the chicken coop."

J.P. said he would before next week. After Jerry left, J.P. let the horses into the pasture, and did they ever enjoy that, for it was a very large pasture of over ten acres. Then J.P. went to his mom's cottage and told her the fences were all done and that he let the horses out to be able to have room to run in the pasture, and said he would make sure to bring them in before dark.

Sara said, "Thank you, honey, and after lunch Heather and I are going into town to do some things, so could you watch after your grandma while we are away? You don't have to be there every minute; it's just in case she needs something."

"Yes, I would be happy to," J.P. said.

So after lunch, Sara and Heather got ready and then got the golf cart out and went to town.

J.P. didn't know it, but his grandma told Sara to fix a bank account for J.P. of about $10,000, so he could have money to spend while living there at the farm.

While Sara and Heather were going to town in the golf cart, Heather said, "Grandma, I love it more and more staying here with all of you."

Mary helped Sara find a golf cart, so she could get around better and not have to drive the Rascal. It was not big enough for bringing things home from town. She knew that her son was home now, so she needed her independence to go where she wanted to go.

First off was the bank, and they both went inside and talked about setting up an account for her son, and the teller told one of the bank reps to help Sara, and Sara signed a lot of papers for her son's new account. Then she set up a small account for her granddaughter as well, to give her a nice start in life.

Heather was very surprised about this, and they both left after this was done, and Sara said, "Your dad will be having a birthday soon, on the 22nd of June, and I will be ordering a cake for him. Do you know what his favorite cake is?"

Heather said, "Chocolate."

Sara said, "I will order it early today, so it will be ready to pick up on Saturday, since everything is closed on Sunday."

They both went into the bakery and ordered the cake and some goodies for breakfast, and then left. The next stop was the feed store, to have them send out some horse feed and some hay until they were able to plant hay in the other area of Sara's property.

They went to the pet store because she needed a large bag of Amberli's favorite dog food and some bird seed as well. Then she saw an orange canary and asked what the price was.

The owner said, "He's on sale for fifty dollars."

Sara said, "I will take him, and also some canary feed. Does he sing a lot?"

The owner said, "Yes, he does, and you will enjoy his song very much."

After the pet store, they went to the general store and got a lot of food items, and then they went to the hardware to order materials to build a chicken coop.

When they were all done, Sara asked Heather what she planned to do when she got out of school.

"Heather said, "I'm not really sure yet, so I may just forgo college and work for a while, whatever I like doing the best. If this pans out, I may start my own business in town."

"That sounds good," said Sara. "Let's go to the diner and have some iced tea and some kind of snack. How does that sound?"

"Great, Grandma. I am craving something sweet."

They drove to the diner and parked and went inside. Cindy greeted them and found an empty table for them and gave them menus.

Sara said, "You don't have to have iced tea; you can have whatever you want."

"Oh grandma, I would like a chocolate malt and a piece of banana cream pie."

Sara said, "I am going to have iced tea and lemon pie."

So they got their orders and enjoyed their snacks in silence. Afterwards, they left a tip and paid, then said goodbye to Cindy and left.

"Now, Heather, we have one more place to go. It's Sally's Lace, to get you some clothes for the summer."

When Heather heard this, she almost jumped out of the golf cart with joy.

When they got to the dress store, they went in and Sally said, "Welcome. How can I help you today?"

"Well," Sara said, "this young lady needs summer clothes and a bathing suit, if you have any in stock."

"Sure," Sally said, "I will take Heather and help her find what she wants."

Sara said, "Wonderful. I will sit here and rest while you two are busy finding some nice things to wear."

While Sara was waiting, a lady came in and saw Sara sitting there, and introduced herself as the teacher at the junior high school nearby. Her name was Katherine.

Sara asked, "When does school start in town?"

Katherine said, "The last of August, and before this there is a fair in the next town."

Sara said, "This is wonderful. So it gives the students something fun to do before they go back to school."

Katherine said, "That's right."

Sara asked, "When will I be able to register my grandchild in school?"

Katherine said, "Two days before school starts."

Sara asked, "Is there any group of teens she can get to know before this?"

Katherine said, "Yes. They are at the city park. Two times a week they have summer projects and crafts for them. Do you think she would be interested?"

"Yes," Sara answered as Heather walked up to Sara to model her new outfit. Sara said, "Wow, that's really a cute outfit." She told Katherine that Heather was from Houma, Louisiana. They were introduced and then Katherine said the teens meet on Tuesday and Thursdays.

Soon they were done and Sara paid for everything and then they left after saying thank you and goodbye. They were both so happy for all of the things they found out today. As they drove home, Heather said, "This is so cool to find a place I can go and enjoy the summer."

Sara said, "That's true, and also, the county fair in the next town is coming up in August, and we all can go to that, if you would like to."

Heather said, "If I get to know some teens, I may go with them, if it's all right."

Sara said, "That would be fine."

Finally, they got home to the cottage and J.P. came out and helped bring everything inside. He said, "This looks like you bought everything in town," and he laughed. Then he drove his mom's golf cart to the shed and plugged it in for her.

"It is so nice to have someone help me, for a change."

Then her mom said, "It's hard for me to get around any more" and giggled.

J.P. came back in and said, "Mom, I am going to take a walk and see the couple down by the lake, and see if they need anything. I won't be too long."

Sara said, "Sure. You go right ahead, for I need to relax for a while. Then I will start supper for all of us."

Heather then said, "I am going to go to the cottage and put my new things away. It's so neat that Grandma did this for me today."

"Sure, Heather, you just relax and enjoy yourself. Bye."

As J.P. was walking to the cabin, he said to himself that he liked this new life with his Mom. As he got to the cabin, the couple came to greet him and asked what they could do for him.

He said, "I wanted to see if you needed help with anything before you move to be with your family."

They said no, because it was all taken care of. "In two weeks could all of you come and see us off?"

J.P. said, "Sure we can."

The couple said, "We are giving you the key to our cabin by the lake, and we want to show you something before you go home."

J.P. said, "Okay."

So they took him to the jetty by the lake and inside the boathouse was a boat for going fishing in on the lake. J.P. was so pleased to see this. He was used to boats because he had worked on a shrimp boat in Houma, Louisiana.

They said, "This is for you, as well as the cabin for helping your mother in her time of need. We have one more surprise."

J.P. asked himself *what could top this?*

"There is someone who wants to meet you in person after all of these years for the first time."

Soon a craft from the sky landed in the field near the cabin, and the door opened and a man on crutches came down the ramp and introduced himself.

"I am your true father, and your mother tried to tell you about me, because you wondered who your father was. I am he."

J.P. was so happy, and tears ran down his cheeks as he gave his dad a hug.

Then his dad said, "Once a month I will come here to this cabin and visit with you, and give you instructions and tell you what your mission is, and what your star name is. I can't stay long, because I am going to the hospital ship to get some legs to walk with. You see, they have a way of taking a cell from your body and putting it in a

Petri dish, and it will form new legs, and then I can walk without crutches. But you already know how I lost the ones I have. I have a gift for you."

Then his father handed him a golden pendant with a ruby and a moonstone in the middle of a pyramid. "You must wear this all the time, for it will keep you safe. Well, it's time for me to go now," and his father went back inside the craft and the door closed and lifted up and flew off very fast.

"Well," was all J.P. could say at the moment. Then he said to the couple, "I must go now," and he gave them each a hug and thanked them. They would all be here to see them off in two weeks.

So J.P. went back to the cottage, and when he got there, he realized he had better bring the horses to the barn for the night. He got busy with doing that. After all the horses were safe in their stalls, he went to his mom's house, where everyone was ready to eat.

They all said a blessing and ate supper in silence. This had been a very busy and exciting day for everyone, and so they all went to bed early after helping Mom clean the kitchen.

CHAPTER 8

MEANWHILE — BACK AT my cottage — I was up early, because I wanted to get some extra things done in the garden. Before I went outside I decided to let Sparkle and her puppies outside in the fenced yard, so they could explore what it was like in the outside.

Some walked out and I carried the others out. They were getting really cute as they got bigger and were ready to play; even the runt of the litter was a little stronger now. I still had not named her because I wanted to see if she would make it or not. The puppies were now over a month old.

After I carried them outside and put down water for them all, I went back inside, and just as I did, the phone rang. I picked up the phone, and it was Sara. I said, "How are all of you doing over there now with all of those horses?"

Sara said, "Just wonderful. I love my personal horse so much. She is a beauty. She is a red-like color and also is almost ready to give birth. Heather's horse, too, is about to give birth. Her horse is a palomino, and even the little miniature horse is going to give birth." Then Sara said, "What I called about is my son's birthday is on June 22nd, and were going to have a party for him on the 21st. This is because I don't like to give a big celebration like this on Sunday, the day of rest. It will be outside in the garden, and we will cook steaks and hamburgers. This will give my son a chance to meet others about his age. He will be 51. Do you think you can make it?"

I said, "I know I can, and so can my brother and his wife. His sons will be here soon with their wives, and they will be staying in the attic until their homes are built on the property my brother just bought. I will have to ask Dad and Mom what plans they have on that day, and if they are free, then I will call you."

Sara said, "That sounds good to me. It will take place on a Saturday, like I just said."

We said goodbye to one another, and then I went into the garden, where Martha was already at work. "Good morning, Martha. I see you are already into doing the weeding."

"It's a nice day, so I wanted to be out here."

I said, "That's good. It's nice to work and when the two of us can get together, it's even better, because we can talk while we work, and that will make our work go faster."

Martha said, "You are right."

I said, "My friend Sara may need some help, too, because she has over 50 roses that she is keeping in a cool place with water until she is ready to plant them. She has not had a chance since she moved here, because of her son and granddaughter moving in."

"Then let's help her on Monday, because it's Friday now and the weekend is coming up."

"I want to ask you if you and my brother would like to go to Sara's place for a picnic on June 21st, the day before her son's birthday, and I know that your sons and wives will be here on Sunday. They are invited too. No gifts required, just the presence of good friends."

"Sure, we would love to go, and our sons would like this as well as their wives."

I said, "Sara told me that three of the female horses are going to give birth soon, and two of them twins. This is the second time for the two regular size horses, and the first time for the little pony."

Martha said, "I would love to see it when the little pony gives birth. Do you think Sara would let me and your brother witness this?"

I said, "Sure, she would love to have you see the birth. It looks like we are almost done here. I am so happy you are helping me with the garden, Martha."

Martha said, "I love helping you with this because it gets me outside in the fresh air. Oh, I made some sun tea. Would you like a glass when we are done? I have some chilled glasses in the freezer."

Martha said, "Yes, I would love some, and we can go into the Gazebo and relax. Oh, here comes Mike. That's good, for I also made tuna sandwiches for all of us. Well, we're done, so let's get the tea and sandwiches and bring them to the Gazebo."

After Mike and Martha and I washed our hands, we carried everything outside. As we were enjoying our lunch, two cars drove onto the property. "I wonder who that could be."

Four smiling young adults came around the corner of the cottage just then, and they said, "We wanted to surprise you and Dad and Aunt Mary"

Mike and Martha said, "You sure did."

"Am I right in what I am seeing? Are both of you young ladies going to make me a grandma and your dad a grandpa?"

"Yes, you are going to be grandparents."

I said, "I know you are tired from your long trip. Sit down now and I will get some more sandwiches and iced tea."

"Yes, we would love that, Aunt Mary."

"I will be back soon," I said. When I returned with some lunch for the new arrivals, I said, "Mike, you may have to build sooner than expected, and I wonder if we can get a large crew of people to help with this."

Mike said, "I will talk to Dad and see what he has to say about it tomorrow. But in the meantime we can get two large trailers for them to live in until the houses are being built."

Then the two couples said, "Not to worry, we traveled with our own trailers, so all we need is electricity and a place for the sewage."

"We could fix that, by digging a regular place for this. But until it's done, why not have one couple stay in the loft bedroom, for there is a bathroom up there, and the other couple can stay in the attic. There is an outside entrance from there. Now that this is settled, let's enjoy the rest of our lunch."

After this, the men carried the luggage to the place they had chosen, and when they were done, the men went out to the pasture to check on the cows and the other animals, while the women went into the cottage to relax and talk.

I asked them if they and their husbands would like to go to a picnic at my neighbor's house on June 21st for a party for her son. "Oh I forgot. I have to make a phone call to Dad and Mom and tell them you are here and all that good stuff."

Just as I was about to punch in the numbers, the phone rang. It was Dad. I said, "Hello, Dad. This is a surprise. I was just about to call you."

He said, "I have news for you, too."

"You first, Dad."

"Sara just called and said all three horses are starting to give birth. Would anyone like to go and see this?"

"Yes, we would. Martha wanted to see the little pony give birth, since they are miniature horses."

Dad said, "Then come on over. I am at Sara's now and it's about to happen."

I got out the golf cart and the ladies got into it, for it had three double seats. The men saw that we were going, so they sat in the back. We drove right to Sara's barn, where everyone was gathered, and Dad said, "Here comes the first one from Ginger."

It was a male, and soon after, another was born and it was a female. The male was a chestnut color and the female was red like her mother. As soon as they were able, they were trying to stand up on wobbly legs, and then all that were gathered said, "How sweet and cute."

Then the little pony surprised them with twins as well, and they were so small and huggable. Martha said, "I can hardly wait so I can be able to come over and hug them both." With tears running down Martha's cheeks, she said, "Mike, can I get one of these for myself later?"

He said, "Sure, my love, we will go see about some when everything gets all set with the houses, because we will be grandparents in six months, and the parents need a place to live before this happens."

Martha said, "That's okay, I can wait."

The next birth surprised everyone, too. The beautiful palomino gave birth to one male and one female. The female was almost a white color, and the male horse was the same color as the mom.

They were so sweet. Then they all stood on wobbly legs and went to suckle their mom. Heather was so thrilled for her horses to have new ones come into the world, and her father said, "Now remember, you must do your best to make sure these little ones are fed every day during the rest of the summer, until they are big enough to be on their own."

Heather said, "Oh yes, Dad, I will, because this is a dream come true."

Before we all left, Sara talked to my Dad on the side so that no one would hear, and said if he didn't have any plans on June 21st, would he and the rest of the family like to come to a picnic at her place, for it was a surprise birthday party for her son, so that he could get to know everyone.

Dad said, "Yes, we would love to come." Then we all left.

When we all got back to my cottage, I said, "It's good you arrived now."

"Why?" they all chimed in.

"Because I am doing a special Father's Day talk at church Sunday, and now it will be even more special. Well, it looks like we better start cooking, ladies, for we have a lot of family here tonight. Could you three strong men please put the extra leaves in the dining room table?"

They said, "Sure."

Martha said she would go to her cottage and get busy with the cooking of the meat and make some biscuits. I said I would do some potatoes and vegetables and dessert. So one daughter-in-law went with Martha to help and the other one stayed with me. The men were busy setting up the table and chairs and putting a heat-proof pad on the table, and then the tablecloth, and they set the table.

After they were done with this, they brought the cows from the pasture to the barn and did a second milking. They also milked the goats. Afterwards, they put the milk in a cooler for the night. Then they brought Many Stars in, to bed her down for the night with her colts.

Saturday went, and then Sunday came, and we all went to the church on the hill at the glass chapel, and soon it was my turn to give my talk on fathers. After Grace gave her talk, she said, "Mary has a few words about fathers.

"I am so happy today because I have my whole family that will be making a new life in this wonderful town," I began.

"Fathers are many things to all of us. They keep a roof over our heads when we are young. Our heavenly Father does much the same thing, for he has many children not only from our beautiful planet, but other worlds as well. Heavenly Father protects all of us from harm, just like our earth father protects us from getting into trouble, even after he warns us not to do a certain thing. He loves us, no matter what kind of a life we lead, because he is our father and he forgives us always. Some are new to being fathers, and some will soon be fathers. No matter what life may bring to any of us, all we have to do is talk to him and he will guide us with his words of knowledge.

"So before we all go today, let's all stand up and give our father a great big hug. And, Dad, I love and respect you so very much, and this will never end."

After this, we all got up and hugged our fathers. Then we sat down and Grace gave a prayer and then told us all to turn to a special song about fathers. "Now rise up from your seat, and let us all sing *Father, this hour has been one of joy.*"

Father, this hour has been one of joy; We thank thee
For thy many blessings. Our hearts are filled with
thy greatest love and thy tender caring.

After the song, we gathered our things and began leaving the chapel, and then went outside and wished everyone well for a nice Father's Day. Soon, one by one, we all drove home.

Martha and the two daughters-in-law were fixing a special meal for everyone. After they ate, I brought out the gift I made for my father. It was a framed poem I did by embroidering it for my father. He opened it and he was so touched that tears ran down his cheeks. This is what was said:

You have Father above and a Father on Earth.
This love is eternal, and always life-giving.
When danger is upon us, an umbrella of his arms covers us.
That is why he will never leave us.
Love, Mary

The next week was a busy one for people to gather and to get together on the building of the two homes. Then it was Saturday again of June 21st. Sara was very busy getting everything set up for the party for her son, and she went to town to pick up the cake. They were going to have a barbecue in the garden for everyone. This was not an easy task, keeping it from her son, but she did her best. It was not fancy because this was a guy thing.

I offered help on this, too, by having one of her nephews take J.P. around and show him things in town, because he, too, needed to know the town, and they even went to see George at his farm, to learn some things about farming.

Then it was time for the party, and the boys came home to Sara's cottage just at the right time. J.P. came into the garden and saw my family and his own family and was truly surprised. He knew that grown men he had known in the past did not cry, because he was told it was not macho to cry, but he didn't care about that now. He was so happy for this get-together for his birthday, it didn't matter anymore.

He found out from his mom that a true man has feelings, and to cry makes a better man. He told everyone thank you for being here and wishing him a happy birthday, because this had never happened to him before. And then the party began.

Everyone ate and talked and got to know one another right away, and there was a lot of laughing and joking as well. Then the cake was brought out and we all sang to J.P. This was a day John would never forget. They all talked and asked what everyone was going to do on the Fourth of July, because that was coming up the next week.

I told all of them that I had heard that a big celebration was going to be held at the town square with a parade and all kinds of fun things going on. There would be food of many kinds and they would top it all off with the fireworks display afterwards. Everyone thought that sounded like fun, so we decided to all gather there. "And let's have a get-together of our own at the park, where we all bring something to eat, like a potluck, you know?"

They all said this was a great idea. Then my family and I left, to go to our different homes, but before we did, we helped to clean up.

That evening before they all went to bed, J.P. told his family that on the Saturday after the fourth of July, the elderly couple wanted the whole family to come to the log cabin to see them off and say their goodbyes. They all agreed that this was a very good idea.

Then J.P. told his family, "I have volunteered to help build the two homes for Mary's family. There are going to be many townspeople to help, too. We hope this will be done before the new babies arrive, for the time of the two births will be December, and this is when the weather changes and gets cold."

Soon they all said a prayer together and hugged good night, and J.P and Heather went to their cottage, and they all went to bed.

The next morning after breakfast, they went to church and then came home because they were still tired after the party and just wanted to be lazy the rest of their Sunday afternoon.

During the afternoon Sara got a call from her brother in Canada, saying he would like to come down for Christmas. Sara said that would be wonderful, "for we can all have a grand time then."

He then also said he would be there until after the New Year, so they set a date to come out, and he said, "Sis, could you make reservations at the bed-and-breakfast for Joyce and me?"

Sara said, "Sure, I would love to. I will call you when I have made the arrangements."

They said their goodbyes and Sara went up to take a nap. As she was sleeping, a voice spoke to her, and said it was Commander Sanni Ceto. Sanni told her that on July 16th there would be a meeting at the little hut by the rapids. "This is where you cross the rope bridge and then walk a little ways to the hut. I want you to bring Mary and Cindy and Grace with you, because this is the first private lesson for the four of you, and I will be giving you some things that will be a project for you to perform. So don't forget now. You must all be there together at 1:00 pm sharp. See you then."

And then Sara fell into a deep sleep. They were all so tired, that after letting Amberli inside, they were not even hungry. So they did not wake up until Monday morning.

The morning was so beautiful that Sara said, "Today I am going to take a walk alone." And then she got a call from me and Martha, that I would be coming over to help her plant those roses. So Sara said, "Oh my, thank you so much."

So after she hung up, she said, "Well, I guess I'll have to wait until later to do my exploring." She was also very hungry and started to get to work on a big breakfast for her family. There was going to be bacon and sausage and eggs, and pancakes and coffee or milk, and, oh yes, fresh squeezed orange juice.

J.P. came in the kitchen then and said all of the horses and colts were in the pasture. After breakfast he was going to town to pick up some things at the hardware store for the chicken coop and then check out some hens to see what kind they had.

Sara said, "I forgot to give you your gift. I am glad I did, because it's better to give your gift in private."

"Mom, there was no need for a gift."

Sara then said, "Yes, there is," and then she handed him an envelope.

He opened it and saw a checkbook and savings book with his name on it, and was so happy that he picked up his mom in a hug and swung her around in the kitchen.

"Not so tight."

Then he said, "Sorry mom, I got carried away." He set her down and said, "Thank you so much, for this really will be a great help for me."

"You are most welcome," Sara said, "and remember, the savings are an IRA for when you retire at age 67, and so you will have some extra to live on with your Social Security."

Sara's mom walked into the kitchen just then with her walker and sat down at the table. Next, Heather walked into the kitchen. They all ate a hearty breakfast, while telling one another what their plans were for the day.

Heather said she was invited to go to a swim party at a lake with her friends and said she would be careful.

Waneta said, "I am going to the garden to sit in the gazebo, and then, if I feel like it, I would like to see how my pony is doing."

Sara asked, "Would you like for me to get the Rascal out for you and put it close to the gazebo?"

Her mom said that would be nice. "Maybe I will go see my pony first, will you help me?"

Sara said, "Sure, of course I will."

After all the dishes were washed and put away, Sara went and got the Rascal out and brought it to the back door, instead of the gazebo, so her mother would not have so far to go. Then, after her mother was in the Rascal, she placed her walker across the basket and had J.P. also take a lawn chair to the pasture fence near the barn, so his grandma, when she got there, could sit and watch all the horses. Then her mother was on her way to enjoy her day.

Heather went and got ready because her friends were coming to pick her up for the swim party, and J.P. got in his truck and went to town.

Just as they left, Sara was alone at last, but then I knocked on her door and Martha and I were there to help to plant the roses in the garden.

So, since there were three of us, the planting got done in no time. After we left, Sara went to see her mom, to see if she needed any help. She then realized that she had to hold off on her walk for a little bit, until her mother got back to the cottage.

In an hour her mom was back at the cottage and smiling from ear to ear.

Sara asked her, "What did you see that makes you so happy today?"

Waneta said, "The two colts and the mama came to the fence and let me pet them and talk to them. They are so sweet and soft to the touch. Honey, will you go and get my walker, so I can come inside?"

Sara said yes. She went to the pasture fence to get the lawn chair and walker. When she returned, she set up the walker so Waneta could come inside. After getting out of the Rascal, her mother said, "Later I will go to the stable, but right now I want a nap."

Then Sara went with her mother to help her into bed, and said, "Will you be all right while I take a walk?"

Her mother said, "I will be just fine; now, you go, and take Amberli, for she has not been on a walk for a while."

So Sara got her walking shoes on and put a leash on Amberli and they were on their way.

As Sara was walking her dog along the dirt road, she came upon a structure that was very different than she had ever seen before, attached to the side of a cave. She saw that no one was there, so she carefully looked inside. Just as she did, she smelled a strong, terrible stench. She covered her nose and walked inside.

What she saw was horrible. She got her flashlight and found a hanky and put this over her nose and mouth, then went inside. And then she noticed, after her eyes were used to the dark, that there were bodies everywhere in different stages of decomposition. This surprised her a little, with a small bit of a shiver, because she had never seen anything like this before. It was just horrible.

She went out right away and realized these men had been miners that were doing things in the cave to either get gold or silver, or whatever they were looking for. But she also saw they had been shot, and then she noticed an opening that looked like a cave, but right away she had to use the cell phone to call the local sheriff. She then waited outside, for she couldn't take any more of the stench.

When the sheriff arrived from nearby, they also had the medical examiner with them from the next town. They went inside the lean-to while Sara stayed outside to not get in the way. After a while, they brought the bodies out in body bags and drove off. The sheriff said, "We do not want anyone to go in there until after the investigation is done by the crime scene investigators. They will be here soon. This is a very grisly crime scene."

Sara said, "I wonder how long they have been here."

He said he was not sure yet, but guessed it was at least a week.

She said, "Can I go home now?"

He said, "Yes, and thank you for calling me, and I am sorry you had to see this. In this town, you see, most of the townspeople are very open when it comes to spiritual things." The sheriff said to her, "I know you are new in town, but I also know you are a true medium. Can you help us with this investigation, because we have only found one fingerprint and not much to go on."

Sara said, "When I find out anything, I will let you know, for this is not something that comes in a hurry. It comes when I least expect it."

"Please let me know what you find out."

Sara turned around and walked back to her cottage with Amberli. When she got home, she opened the door and went inside. She had just sat down with a cup of coffee in the living room and, as she sat there, it came to her that there were more parts of this than she first believed there was. This was going to take a long time to find out who this monster was, but whatever came to her, the first thing would be to call the sheriff about it.

The rest of the week was a blur to Sara because she was thinking about this tragedy. The following week she said she needed to get this horrible thing out of her mind, for she wouldn't be able to enjoy the Fourth of July on Friday.

A voice spoke to her just as she thought this. "This is Yahweh. My child, leave this in my hands and later all of your guides will help you with this mystery."

She thanked him and then soon felt uplifted.

The Fourth of July was busy for everyone, including me and my large family. There was a lot of hustle and bustle going on, to get ready and leave for town. Finally, we were all ready and left. We drove the golf cart, and it was good that we had a compartment in the back for picnic supplies and food.

When we got to the park, we saw Sara and waved at her and her family, and went to see where they had decided to have their picnic. There were about four picnic tables close by that were empty, so we were glad about this, and it was good to also bring some extra lawn chairs between the two families.

Soon the Mayor came to the podium and welcomed everyone to the celebration. "Let the parade begin."

It was a wonderful parade with horse-drawn carriages and people on horseback with all of the red, white, and blue finery, lots of flags waving as the people in the parade walked by.

After this was over, we had all kinds of booths with things for sale and cotton candy and hot dogs and all kinds of other different foods. Everyone was laughing and there was dancing. There was a band playing in the gazebo in the middle of the park. The children played and had a lot of fun chasing one another and playing games. The younger babies were sound asleep, for this was too much for some of them.

The sheriff was there with his family and he excused himself and walked over to Sara. Sara said, "Hi, how are you? Are you having as much fun as my family and I?"

He said, "Yes, we sure are," and then he took her to the side so that no would hear and asked her if anything had come to her yet.

She said, "I did get something, and you may have to have a crew go back out there this next week."

He asked, "Why is that?"

Sara said, "In a dream I saw a lot more bodies that were buried under the floor of the lean-to, and you may have to dig carefully to unearth them."

The sheriff said, "This is very grave indeed. This monster has got to be caught."

Sara said, "Have you gotten any more leads yet?"

Cliff, the sheriff, said, "No, not any more. Let's try not to think any more about this today. Let's enjoy the day. We will talk later."

They both went back to their families. Soon it was getting dark, and the Mayor made an announcement that the fireworks were about to begin. The band then played the music for the fireworks and the fireworks began. There was a different song for each display and it was fantastic as well as beautiful.

When it was over, they gathered and cleaned up after themselves and carried what was left to their cars, or whatever they drove in that day. They all went home.

As soon as all of them were home, they let the dogs in the house and went to bed. They were all pooped from all of the fun they had.

Sara and her family had a nice breakfast the next morning, bright and early Saturday, and would relax for a while before it was time to go to the cabin.

It was soon time to go and see the elderly couple off on their long trip home. They all got into the golf cart and drove to the cabin.

When they got there, the couple said, "Let's go stand by the lake on the jetty." The jetty was just big enough for all of them.

As they stood and waited, all of a sudden a silver spacecraft came up out of the middle of the lake. And everyone just stood staring at it with opened mouths.

The couple then turned and said to all of them, "Well, here's our ride."

They were so in awe because it was hard for them to say much.

Then J.P. said, "Wow, your ride is beautiful."

The rest of the family said, "Yes, it sure is."

Then the craft floated just above the water near the jetty and a door opened that was not there before. The couple gave their hugs and said, "You are a very special family, this is why we chose you to have this cabin. J.P. will be the owner of it and maintain it."

Then a tall being came out with blond hair and blue eyes, and gave all of them a special crystal pendant and a blessing. The elderly couple then went onto the craft, and they waved before the door closed.

As soon as it did, the silver craft rose up and then flew very fast and out of sight within a blinking of an eye.

The family just stood there for a while in awe of it all, then turned around and walked off the jetty and got into the golf cart and drove back to the cottage. They drove home in silence and remained so for the rest of the weekend.

Monday was busy as always, for both my family and Sara's too. Then Sara had a thought about Max and called me. I answered the phone and said, "Hello, Sara, how are you doing?"

Sara said, "Fine. I just called to ask about Max, how is he doing?"

I said, "Not too good, I'm afraid."

Sara said, "Mary, could you put a leash on Max and let's go to the lake and get the rowboat out and go to the area just past the cave?"

I said, "I will meet you in front of my cottage."

Sara was there very soon. We both walked to the special place where we had the boat hidden and got it out of the boathouse and pulled it to the jetty and tied it, and then we got into it. Sara undid the rope and Max sat there in the middle of the boat with his tongue hanging out, and it looked like he was smiling.

As we both rowed the boat, it went past the small special cave, and we saw an inlet just ahead and rowed to the small inlet. Soon we saw some steam just off the shore and there was a small waterfall and the smell of sulfur. We saw a small jetty and tied the boat to the jetty, and all of us got out.

As we walked to the sulfur spring, I said, "What is this all about?"

And Sara said, "I had a dream, and in the dream I was told that this one time Max could get in the water with us, and the water will heal him of his cancer."

I said, "It's worth a try."

We both took off our shoes, and since we were just in shorts, we walked into the spring. As we sat in the water that was nice and warm, I said, "You know what?"

Sara said, "What's that?"

I said, "Even I am starting to feel better."

Sara said, "Me, too. This feels really good."

Then I said, "I'm ready to climb out, how about you?"

Sara said, "Me, too. One more thing I forgot to mention."

I asked, "What is that?"

Sara said, "This spring has also been blessed with more than you may know for healings and it's not just the sulfur. It's something more as a gift from our friends from the stars."

I said, "That is wonderful to know, but we need to keep this to ourselves for a while, until the people in our town are fully awake as to who they are."

Sara said, "Yes, that is so very true."

I said, "Yes, we should."

We got back into the boat after putting on our shoes, and we untied the line and were on our way back. Soon we were at the jetty, where we had left from, and tied it while they got out, and then Sara placed the row boat in the small boathouse. We walked together to my cottage. Then Sara walked back to her cottage. Both of us, when we got home to our own cottages, each made our own lunch and then changed clothes before eating lunch.

At my cottage:

I felt wonderful ever since I got home. I took a shower and changed clothes. I went to the pasture to visit my horse Many Stars. I hoped some day to have a chance to ride my horse. But for today, I just stood there, admiring my beautiful horse and her colts. They were growing fast and were very playful as they ran around the pasture, having a very good time.

After a while, I walked back to the cottage and read my mail. I heard a bark and looked up to see Max happily wagging his tail really fast as he looked in the back door. So I got up and let him in, then sat down again. He came up to me and laid his head in my lap and put his paw on my knee, and then he got up on his two legs in my lap and licked my face.

I said, "What is this? You seem really happy today and you even look better."

For some reason I didn't know, he moved his head to one side, barked, and I said, "Would you like to go and see Skip?"

He barked again. I then went and got the phone and called the vet. When Skip answered, I said, "May I bring Max in today?"

He said, "Is something wrong?"

I said, "It's hard to explain, but all I know is that Max is very cheerful today, for some reason, and I would like to see why he seems this way."

Skip said "Bring him in and we will do some tests."

After I hung up the phone, I got the leash and put it on Max, and we both went out the door. We went to town.

Soon we were there and went in, and as soon as Max saw Skip, he ran over and almost jumped up on Skip and knocked him to the floor to lick his face.

Skip said, "Down, boy," and Max got down. Skip said, "I know what you mean." So he took Max in back and did some tests on him while I waited.

The attendant came in and said, "This may take awhile, so if you have errands to do, this would be a time to do them."

I decided to walk around town. I was nervous a little bit, wondering what Skip was going to find out about Max. It was good that I had my cell phone with me. After a while, it rang and I answered, and Skip said, "You need to come back now because I have some good news for you."

I said I was on my way right now. As soon as I got there, Skip said, "I don't know how to tell you this, Mary, but all of the signs of cancer are gone and Max is in perfect health."

I said, "What? This is a miracle."

Skip said, "He has a slight smell of sulfur on his fur. Where did you go today?"

I had to tell him that Sara and I had gone for a walk and then gotten into a rowboat at the lake and seen an inlet and went down it and then saw some steam vapors in the wooded area, so there was a small jetty and we tied the boat to it, then got out. "We saw this small pool near a small waterfall that trickled down some rocks. We took off our shoes and got into it, and so did Max. It felt wonderful. After a while, we got out and put on our shoes, and Max shook off the water, and then we got in the boat and came home afterwards."

Skip said, "Well, whatever it was in that water, it helped to heal Max so much, he is acting more like a young puppy."

I said, "We can't tell this to the people just yet, because this is a very special place, and I hope you understand. In time, as time goes by, we will take one at a time to this place, as a last resort for their sickness, when there is no cure for their sickness."

Skip agreed to this and said, "The same goes for special pets."

"Yes," I said. I then left and came home to the cottage. It was getting dark, so I made a small dinner for everyone and afterwards went to bed, after I took a shower, because all I did was get dressed today.

As I slept, I saw my friend Anita in my dream, and she gave me a message. "I led you and Sara to that sulfur spring for a healing, and I wanted to give my Max a healing, as well as you and Sara."

I said, "Thank you so much for this. I am truly grateful and so is Max."

Anita said, "You are wise to keep this place to yourselves for a while, for if you let too many in there, the water will loose its strength."

I said, "I understand," then was fast asleep again with no dreams after talking to Anita.

While Sara was feeling really good herself and had a very nice good night's sleep, the next morning after she got up and was in the kitchen starting coffee, her mother came into the kitchen, but this time without her walker. Sara said, "Mom, how come you are no longer using your walker? Don't you think you should, so you don't fall?"

Her mother said, "I don't need it anymore. I have been healed in my right leg and right arm from my long case of the stroke all these years."

Sara then ran and hugged her mother, and said, "This is so wonderful, for now you can do things you have always wanted to do."

"Yes, I am happy."

Sara said, "We must celebrate tonight. Let's all go out to eat this evening. How would that be?"

Sara's mother said, "It would be wonderful to go out and eat without this darn walker."

Soon Sara's son and granddaughter came in the room and said, "Grandma, you aren't using your walker. What happened?"

Then her son said, "I think that I have the answer to this for all of us. Remember when we all went to see the elderly couple off in the spaceship the other day? The tall people from the craft gave us a pendant and also a blessing that day, and even I am feeling much better than I have in a very long time. This is truly wonderful for all of us."

Sara said that she was planning to have them all go to a restaurant in town and have a celebration for being cured at long last. They all said "here, here" to that. Then they all went out to eat and really enjoyed themselves.

The next day Sara's mother was so chipper that after breakfast she went out to see her pony and two colts, and this time she walked inside the pasture with them. The horse Ginger came up to her and nuzzled her for a hug on the neck. Waneta had some sugar cubes and gave them some sugar. Then the other horses came, too, and wanted some, so it was good she had brought a bagful.

She was having a great time out there with all of the horses, and they were very gentle with her. One of them even kneeled down on the ground for her to get on her back, because Waneta was very short. She then did this, and realized this horse was special in color, and she knew then and there, this horse *chose* her. The horse then stood up and gave Waneta a ride on her back. She held onto her neck.

As she was doing this, J.P. and Sara and Heather came out to the pasture to see what was going on, and for some reason they had brought a camera. Unknown to Waneta, they took pictures of everything that happened. J.P. also had a movie camera with him and was recording all of this.

As Waneta made a second round of the pasture on bareback with her newfound friend, Maple (she had named her), she noticed everyone watching her, and she smiled a big smile and waved with one hand. Then she told Maple she wanted to get down now and thanked her for the ride.

To everyone's surprise, the horse kneeled and let Waneta off her back. She said as she got off Maple, "That was the most fun that I have had in all of my life, being on the back of this wonderful, gentle, loving horse." Then they all hugged her and J.P. literally carried her back to the cottage.

The color of this horse was tan with a grey mane and grey spots on the rump. They all said that now they could all go riding together soon. "Won't that be fun?" Yes, they all said.

Then Sara's mother said, "Would it be possible for me to have a carriage placed on my little pony, so that I can get used to having her pull me with my weight, for I would like to be in a parade at Christmas time, and it would be fun to ride in the snow with a blanket on my knees."

"Yes, we will help you learn how to handle the carriage."

CHAPTER 9

THE WEEKS WENT BY and it was soon July 16th. Sara wanted to make sure everyone was going to be on time for the meeting at the hut for their first lesson, so she made some calls to let them all know.

Before that Saturday, the sheriff came by and told Sara what they had found. They had dug up about seven other bodies. He then said they also discovered the reason why that person had blown up the cave entrance. Cliff said after they carefully dug through the rocks and wooden braces for the mine, they reinforced the beams so it was safe to go farther and look. Then, to their surprise, they saw an underground base with jail-like cells and cages, with very strange beings in them, and a laboratory that had been used for experiments.

Sara then said, "What do they look like, and were there any still living?"

Cliff said, "There were over a hundred of them in these prison-like cells."

"Who else saw this?"

Cliff said, "Only me and my seven deputies."

"Did you alert the government yet?"

He said no.

"That's good," said Sara. "These beings must be released and set free, so they can go home."

Cliff agreed.

Sara said, "Now I have to make some contacts with my guides, to bring the crafts down here tonight, to recover these people. Were there any strange-looking type guards there as well?"

Cliff said, "They were dead."

Sara said, "That's good, because they are terrible beings. I will need your help when the crafts arrive."

Cliff said, "Yes, I will help as well as my deputies."

Sara said, "I have to make some calls to some people and will let you know what to do later."

"Thank you so much for telling me this and not going to the authorities."

He said, "You are most welcome," then said goodbye and left.

Sara called the Commander Sanni Ceto and told her what the sheriff had found and all the details as well, and that there were fifty Pleiadians that had been locked up down there as well as fifty other beings, and a spacecraft was needed tonight to come down and take them to their home worlds.

Sanni said, "We will be there tonight. Commander Khinyeo will be there, too, and also Commander Neron and his crew."

"The sheriff and his deputies will be here to help as well tonight. And you know, I hope that these men, when they go home, will be rewarded for helping with this when it's their time to go home."

"Yes, they will," said Sanni.

That night, about 12:00 AM, they were all gathered, as well as Grace and Cindy and me, to observe this great event. Soon the crafts came down. Commander Khinyeo came up to Sara, and they both hugged in the Zeti way, by putting their hands on each other's shoulders and touching each other's foreheads.

As it turned out, there were more than just fifty Pleiadians and fifty other beings. There were one hundred of each of them. It was a good thing there were more than just two spacecrafts that came. There were several, because of not only taking the live ones, but also the dead ones.

Commander Neron came up to Sara and gave her a very loving hug. Then they started to bring these poor souls onto the crafts, and after each was filled, they took off. They found some living reptoids and they were restrained and taken aboard the penal colony craft, and then they, too, took off.

The last craft to leave was Neron's and Sanni's crafts. This was truly an eventful night. As they left, the people on the ground were told to back up as far as possible, because this cave with the base was going to be sealed with volcanic fluid and it would be very hot. So then they did this, and a large boulder was placed in front of it.

After this, all who were there to help went home, and all knew that, at least for now, they could feel a little safer. Sara knew she had to find this reptoid that had shape-shifted as a human as soon as she was able, and get him removed as soon as possible from Planet Earth and this nice town.

We all had a lot to do before our meeting on July 16th. The time went by fast, and it was almost that time, and we were all getting excited because this was very special for the four of us. It was finally the day, and we all met at my cottage and walked to where the rope bridge was, then crossed it.

We only walked a little ways after getting off the bridge and were soon at the hut. We then climbed, with the help of the rope, and were soon inside the hut. None of us said a word because we were in a special meditative state.

We all sat down and just sat there for a while in deep silence. Then a breeze went by and a craft landed by the clearing. We could see from the corner of our eyes a triangle-shaped craft, and a being came out and walked in. All we could do was sit there in awe, and then the Commander Sanni Ceto told us:

"I thank you for being on time for your first lesson." As she spoke it was done by telepathy. "Let us begin. There will be many things happening on your world that may frighten some. This is true, but it is the unknown that you must learn not to have any fear of. Some of you do not have this fear, and that's very good, but some others do.

"When we do our many missions here on Earth, we have to be brave, and with strong courage, because we are here to help those of whom are not awake as of yet. We have to set an example for them. That's why this first lesson is so very important, for you all are to teach this to others as well. I must now go, and we will meet again in the fall. I give you all a special blessing for having the courage to work together on this important first lesson and path. Farwell, now, and be with God as you walk."

And she was gone.

This was a Wednesday, and Cindy had taken the day off, so she could be at this very special meeting. She did not regret a moment of it.

Grace spoke up and said, "I am so honored that I could be here to have this lesson and witness this sitting and meet the Commander Ceto for the first time. This will help me a lot as I work with people to help them awaken more in our church. I, too, say this has been an honor for me, and I will start with my family as I teach us all to stop having so much fear."

Sara said, "This is a lot simpler for me, because we have had the honor to see our neighbors off when they left in a spacecraft to go home. Well, let's soak our feet for a few minutes in the water, and then we can head home."

I said, "Oh, this feels so good. It's as if we were getting a special treatment at the beauty shop." Then we all chuckled. Soon after this, we all got up and dried our feet and put our shoes back on, then climbed down and went back to our homes.

On Saturday, Sara wanted to take a walk alone and just meditate, so she walked up the road past the lean-to, and saw a nice clearing where there was a small brook, and she decided to stop there and rest. As she was resting, suddenly she was jerked out of it by a man's voice.

He said, "I guess you thought I would be long gone, didn't you, little lady?"

Then a strong voice in her head said, "Warning. Put a stronger shield around you. This is *not* a good person."

She then said thank you to the voice and did as she was told. It was Commander Neron. He said, "I will do the same for you."

After doing this, she turned around and saw a menacing person, and he grabbed her and dragged her to her feet. "You are going with me, and no one will ever hear from you again, *ever*. I know who you are. You will not keep us from your planet."

Sara remembered what the Commander Sanni Ceto had said in that talk about fear a few days ago. She said, "I am *not* afraid of you one bit."

He said, "You better be, because you are going to *die*, because I will *not* let you continue to teach and help the humans anymore."

Sara said, "What is your name?"

He snarled at her and said, "What does it matter to you, Miss Goody Two Shoes?" Then he said, "Well, I am a high commander of my fleet. I am Derectus Dicto."

"Well, you won't get away with all of the vile things you have done," said Sara.

"Oh, but you are wrong, for I have a lot of power and you can't stop me."He then shape-shifted to his true self, one of the Deracs, which are the worst reptoids of them all. He then tried to kiss her with his ugly forked tongue, and tried to rip the clothes off of her.

She yanked away from him and kicked him in the crotch area, and as he was bending over, she zapped him with the three beams and stunned him for a minute.

When this happened, he said, 'What do you think you're doing?" He could not move, because he was surrounded with the pink beam. Reptoids can't handle anything that's loving.

Neron told her, "The ship from the penal colony is on the way as I am talking to you, and I, too, am holding a beam on this outlaw, and all of the commanders are as well. Are you all right, my love?"

"Yes, I know you are with me close by."

The reptoid said, "You will *not* get away with this! Never, Never, Never! You will see."

Sara then said, *"You* will see. Hate is not the answer as well as murder that you have committed. Everyone has to pay a price for their bad deeds."

"I shall never admit to any crime," he told her. "They will have to kill me first."

Then Sara saw a large craft land, and some big beings that were guards got out and put chains on this monster and took him to their ship. He tried to struggle to get away, but could not because they gave him a stunning shot to keep him from moving.

Finally, the door shut and the craft lifted up and went away.

Sara said, "Thank you, my love, for helping me."

Neron said, "This is what I do for my beloved. And soon we will meet for a private time in the future."

And after this, she felt a lot better and walked home. As she did, she said to herself, "Now I have to repair my shirt that he tore, but that's a small price to have to pay. I am still alive. I feel that our town will be much safer from things like this in the future." Then she thought, "I have to call Cliff and tell him and his deputies the news, and I feel it will close this case for good. A lot has happened since I moved here, but I am glad I am safe for now. This is another lesson that I will teach our group, to be careful who we meet in the outside world, and to be very watchful in our daily lives of those who try to scam us in every way."

When she got home, she gave all of her family a big hug and explained what had happened to her. Sara then told them to be very watchful of strangers.

They all were glad that Sara was safe and back with them. Later. Sara called Cliff and told him what happened, so he could alert his deputies about this.

He said, "I think our whole town must put a shield around us to keep us safe. And now this case is closed officially. Bye now."

When Sara called me and told me this, I was in shock for a minute, and then said, "You could have been killed!"

"Yes, I know, but I could not give this monster the benefit of the doubt that I was a little scared because they feed on fear. Thank God it's over. I wanted to ask if, some day soon, you would like to go horseback riding together? I have wanted to ride my horse ever since I got her."

I said, "You know, I, too, have wanted to ride Many Stars as well. When would you like to go?"

"Saturday, if you would like to."

We set up the time and were very excited about our first ride together.

Sara then called Grace and told her what happened, and Grace, too, was in shock. Grace then said, "I think this Sunday would be a good time to start our lessons on fear. Don't you agree?"

Sara then agreed.

The next call was to Cindy and, as before, the same reaction was felt by Cindy, and then she said to Sara, "Could you come to town and have lunch with me on my lunch break?"

Sara said, "Sure, of course."

After supper, Sara's family all went to bed early, because they really needed some time to think alone about the lesson Sara had taught them today.

The next morning was a Friday and they all ate a nice breakfast, did their duties, and then went and enjoyed the day with their friends. Even Sara's mother had a day planned. Some ladies from the church were coming by to take her for a ride in the country, and she was really looking forward to this. It was a blessing that she did not have to use her walker any more. This made life a lot better for her.

Sara, too, got ready and took the golf cart to the diner at noon time to have lunch with Cindy. When she got there, Cindy was waiting for her in the diner. They had a wonderful talk and Sara said to Cindy, "I am so lucky to be living in this town of Welcome Home, because I now feel like I am where I have always wanted to be. My whole family is truly blessed."

Cindy said that since she had been here for several years now, she had no desire to move anywhere else. They were done eating, so Sara left to go home. For some reason, Sara had to call their group that evening, because she felt a need to be together with all of them. She already knew that I was going horseback riding with her, but decided to call Cindy and Grace as well.

After she called them, she was glad that she did, for they all had the same feeling. Sara asked her son afterwards if, in the morning, he could saddle up Ginger and then two other horses for her in the morning. He said he would.

The next morning, Cindy and Grace were early and they all had backpacks on and food for their lunches and water. J.P. helped the ladies onto their horses, and his mom, too, and then they were on their way to my cottage.

When they got to my cottage, I was in front, waiting for them. As they approached, I started to lead the way to the special meadow that I had a dream about a few months ago. This was a beautiful day, and they all were having a leisurely time of it as they went down the road.

When we got to the meadow, we turned our horses into the meadow and walked slowly into it. Soon, just as in my dream, we saw some young cubs playing in the tall grass. We looked around slowly and saw the mother close by. We went in a different direction and rode a different way. We saw a river with a slow flow to it and decided this was a nice place to stop and have a lunch.

We dismounted our horses and let them get some water to drink from the river and then graze in the grass while we had our lunch. The horses were well trained, so they did not go far and stayed nearby. We spread out our blankets to sit on, and got our lunches and sat down and just enjoyed the view from where we were sitting.

It was spectacular with the purple of the distant mountains looking toward Crater Lake. We could barely see the deep blue of the lake, and there was snow on top of the mountains. The sky was so blue and there were no clouds. We ate in silence, for this was so nice to just relax. This was nature at its best.

I was the first to break the silence and I proposed that we get together, whenever the weather allowed, to enjoy our friendship. Cindy said, "I second that. Life is always too short to always be rushing about all the time. It has been so long since we have joined together as friends."

Grace said that our lives have many ups and downs, and we all need to regroup within each one of us, because we just never know what may happen around the bend.

It was Sara's time to talk. She was thinking of what could have happened and we all need to be more aware of what is around us and without fear. "Slowly seek out carefully wherever we go that is not familiar to each of us, first, before we approach an area."

"Yes," we all chimed in.

We packed up our things and took a walk to the river. It was almost like the river was singing to us in a happy tune of being free to flow, as if nothing was in our way. Soon we were all caught up in the song as well as mesmerized by it all.

This is a little of what we felt:

We are free flowing as we go along, we are the stream of the cold as we join it, and part of it. We flow with no cares, to reach wherever we may lead to the sea and then the sun and the clouds take up the moisture of the water and then turn it into rain. And then we start all over again. What a glorious way to be without a care to bother thee.

Soon we all came out of it and noticed some objects in the rivers that were shining. We each picked one up as if we knew the object was just for us. Each of the items was of pure gold. The one Sara picked up was a triangle shape and had a sun in the middle of it and a gemstone which was amber.

Cindy was next, and hers was with a sun in the middle, too, and it was topaz. Then Grace picked hers up, it was a triangle, too, and had a sun in the middle, and the gemstone was a sapphire.

I was last, and mine was a little different than the rest. I was told not to reveal what was on it just yet. There was a marking on the back of Sara's and a symbol of the phoenix, and three more gemstones. It was very powerful. The stones were green and purple and blue in a triangle.

After this, we all mounted up on our horses and turned around and went home. Unknown to us, each object had a special lesson and message for us when we got to our homes.

When we got to my cottage, we all said goodbye and told one another we would see each other at church in the morning. The rest continued to Sara's cottage, and J.P. was there and helped them down, then took the horses to the barn to remove the saddles and put them away. After that, he left them in the corral.

Cindy and Grace had come together in Cindy's car, so after they said goodbye to Sara and thanked her for the use of the horse, they were on their way as well. It was getting dark, so Sara started supper, and afterwards went to bed, as did the rest of the family.

Sunday morning was nice, and the family had a nice breakfast together, and got ready for church. Then they all went to church. The service was a mellow one as they all stood outside afterwards and just held hands and looked out over the valley they lived in.

They were so grateful for the close friendship of all of the townspeople. Each of them knew that even more adventures would be had in the future, and they were thankful to be able to have this gift from Yahweh, because he called them all to gather here as a family. This was the place they were supposed to be, and they all knew, deep in their hearts.

Whatever was to happen in the future, no one knew, but they would savor it with open arms.

They all started to leave and some went to the farm of George and Georgia's for a potluck, like they did every Sunday. This was a tradition that would always stay the same.

In closing this first book I have ever written, I just want to say that there are many stories to come in the future, and many adventures to explore together. So for now, this is the end, but then... is it really? Who knows?

THE END